Just Call Me John

Kevin Mark McCartney

DEDICATION

To Donna May

(My wife, my best friend, and my soul mate.)

CONTENTS

Look Within

~~ACKNOWLEDGMENTS~~

INDICTMENTS

The following persons are partially to blame
for the publication of this manuscript.

My youngest son, Benjamin:
an extraordinary musician and lyricist in his own right,
who served as my sounding board throughout the progression
of this journal and tricked me into believing it was worth completing.
Another of my sons, Ryan: a talented and burgeoning young writer if I may
say so myself, who first encouraged (and helped) me to pen my narrative.
And while I'm at it, I may as well implicate the rest of my amazing family,
for loving, supporting and enabling me despite myself.
Nor can I let escape Mr. Russell M Burden:
author and musician extraordinaire; my long-term writing partner,
iron sharpener, and longer-term dear friend.
(See now, Russ, this is the monster you have helped create.)
Also John - yes, there really is a John: my email Sensei and an unsung hero;
one of the few persons who responds to my messages
even though I still don't own a cell phone.
(John is a much better raconteur than I, truth be told,
though he'll never take credit. We are under a shared oath,
in fact, never to reveal one another's pennames until we both have died -
which contains a bit of a logistical conundrum, as I think about it.)
Last but not least, it is with deep affection that I
must both inculpate and elevate my beloved friend,
Mr. Leonel Cordeiro Agostinho (12/27/1948 - 9/6/2016),
for teaching me the true meaning of generosity and humility,
and showing me what it feels like to both find and then lose
such a deeply cherished friend within so short a time.
(Saudades!)

:: Posting #1 ::

A Brief History of Me

Just call me John.

Everybody else does.

It might even be my name, for all I know. (I wish I did know…)

Which leads to the sole reason I have decided to jot down my memories. For why, you might ask, should a young man of … let's say … about 25 years of age be so prematurely inclined to script his memoirs? A very astute observation on your part, I would note, and one which I'll do my best to answer. (And no, I'm not dying – at least no faster and no more predictably than anybody else of my guesstimated age.)

Part of my enigma, you see, is that my memories only extend a few months back. Before that, nothing. Nada. Blank slate. Empty canvas. Corpus absentia. You get the picture - or the absence thereof.

Just recently I learned - or more likely rediscovered - how to use a computer, and it didn't take long for me to stumble upon one of those social networking sites (namely, this one) where countless persons seem to enjoy blogging and twittering incessantly about themselves … or whatever the technical term might be for publicly sharing one's random thoughts and intimate personal details and activities with family, friends, and, as seems quite likely, a good many strangers as well. That's when my epiphanous plan began to form. (I'm not even sure what that term means, to be honest; it just sort of popped into my head.) Why should I not join them? What if I took advantage, that is to say, of one of these vastly populated social media sites to share what I *do* know and remember about myself? If photographs should not suffice, then perhaps, through this open process of self-characterization, I might reveal some subtle personal detail, flaw, quirk, or

1

attribute that would stir a latent spark of recognition within somebody else, who might then help me to achieve what I have thus far failed to do on my own: discover who I am. Or at least, who I was…

Yes, you would also be correct in saying I'm just another lost soul trying to find himself (I continue to be slightly unnerved by your perceptiveness). But in my case, it might help if I had some vague conception of who it was that I lost, and hence who it is that I'm supposed to be seeking.

So, if you have a few minutes to spare and are feeling rather charitable, grab yourself a cup of coffee and pull up a chair, for I have a peculiar tale that I must share.

:: Posting #2 ::

A Bleak Self Portrait

I acknowledge, as should seem obvious, that I am no writer, and nor do I play one on TV…although I do happen to be writing this from within my cozy room at a Holiday Inn Express, as goes the coincidental commercial playing in the background. (Hotels are my preferred form of habitation, you see, whenever I'm not cruising around in my ridiculously expensive RV.) Nevertheless, I hope to compensate for my lack of eloquence through a spirit of candor. In other words, I'll not try and embellish the details of my life, such as I know them, nor smooth over any of their rough edges; for this would merely defeat my purpose in sharing them in the first place. If nothing else, in consequence of this openness and transparency, you may find yourself occasionally amused at my expense or even embarrassed on my behalf - as is the case with my most faithful and tolerant of companions, who is now resting in an adjoining room.

But I'm leaping ahead of myself; I'm supposed to be looking backward.

Perhaps I should start with my physical description - though I seriously doubt whether *that* will provide much in the way of enlightenment. I'm of average height, average weight, average bleach-blond hair, average Caucasian-American tanned complexion, average facial features, average male-pattern facial hair distribution (currently mustached and bearded), with no distinguishing deformities, piercings, prosthetics, or protuberances. No visible scars or birthmarks (and yes, I do have a bellybutton), and no beauty marks or artistic embellishments, either natural or man-made. Not even a tattoo. - At least I don't think so; I can't honestly recall looking at my own behind of late. Hold on a minute…

No, no tattoos. (Wow, now *that* was rather frightening. Here's a free tidbit, as a reward to you if you're still reading: I wouldn't recommend squatting butt-naked on a mirror as a means of trying to explore your background. In hindsight, so to speak, it's just not worth it.)

Actually, though, this exercise has not proven entirely fruitless, for I've discovered something completely new about myself: I have a small, crescent-shaped mole on my left lower cheek. (Yes, the one you sit on mirrors with, not the one you shave.) But hopefully *that* is not the one detail which will spark somebody's memory.

There, that's pretty much it, insofar as my general appearance is concerned. That should narrow things down quite a bit; I should expect about 40 million leads based upon this verbal composite alone.

I'll attach an actual photograph (of my face, that is) once I've figured out how to do so, which may prove a bit more helpful - though probably no more appealing.

:: Posting #3 ::

First Memory

The earliest memory I can now recall, with any degree of clarity, is of waking up in a strange hotel room - not unlike the one in which I am currently abiding. (Which may be why I keep revisiting them periodically, come to think of it, even though my RV is far more luxurious than most: they are the closest thing I know to returning to the safety of the womb; the humble place in which I was reborn. Or maybe it's just the maid service and the freshly laundered bedsheets…)

The television was blaring out some movie which, judging by its soundtrack, I now believe to have been Grosse Pointe Blank. The song *"I Can See Clearly Now"* is distinctly memorable, as its rhythm was keeping pace with a bounding headache. It also struck me as being a tad ironic, even then, since a walloping thunderstorm was raging outside (competing with the noise from the TV), and my own vision was anything but clear.

I must have lain there for quite some time in my queen-sized bed, enveloped within a tangled mound of blood-stained sheets and blankets; trying to sort out my similarly disheveled thoughts. I was reluctant to get up, due partly to the extreme pain and fuzziness inside my head, but also because I hadn't the foggiest notion about who, let alone where, I was, and hence no clear direction as to where I ought to be going.

Eventually what forced me to get up was a pressing need to urinate, and I fought through waves of vertigo as I navigated, instinctively, towards the bathroom. (My power of recollection was shot to shreds, but I retained the ability to perform those basic, intuitive tasks which we typically do by rote. I had not, in other words, regressed to an infantile state - though some who have since been exposed to my brand of humor may beg to differ. But no matter, I have plenty of excuses at my disposal.)

The face staring back at me from the bathroom mirror looked dazed and unfamiliar. Being caked and splattered with dirt, sand, and a disturbing amount of dried blood probably didn't help matters any, so I washed it off as best I could with some soothing cold water from the sink: dabbing gently at my various encrustations, while tracing the main source of the original bleeding to a nasty spot at the center of my forehead. This wound was broad but not too deep, indicative of some blunt yet forceful trauma. Fresh blood still oozed from it, though not at an alarming rate. (I suspect now that I had suffered a severe concussion, compliments of whatever had collided with my thick skull, but I was too disoriented then to seek medical attention.) My throat was also burning, and after dousing it with the same cool water, I glanced once more into the mystical mirror upon the wall. This time I experienced a vague sense of déjà vu, though I still could not attach a name to that mangy face.

By then I felt as though I might black out at any moment, so I stumbled back to bed - the second of the two, nearest the draped window; the bedding of which was still neat and unsullied.

I had pulled the plug to the TV along the way and was lulled almost instantly back to sleep by the now unrivaled sounds of the howling storm.

I don't know how long I dozed again after that, but when I reawakened, the lyrics to the song I had originally heard seemed now to have come to pass: for the rain had stopped, and my vision had begun to clear.

This time I managed to walk about the room without feeling like I might faint with every footstep. I stood first before the broad, front window and pulled back its heavy curtain.

Day One was heavily overcast but some stray rays of sunlight shone down from a gap in the clouds and lit gloriously upon a shimmering sea, casting a circular spray of diamonds upon its surface.

My hotel room was on the second floor overlooking a beach which I later discovered to be in Cape May, New Jersey. There were no personal items aside my beds, but in the closet, I found a large leather handbag. Inside this bag, in crisp, clean bundles of $100 bills, were three million dollars in cash, along with a pouch-full of precious stones befitting the coffers of any sovereign king – though I could not yet grasp the enormity of these riches.

Of far greater value to me was a small photo-album containing my only clues to a forgotten past. The photographs (forty-two, to be exact, which happened to coincide with the number of gemstones) were of various landscapes – though whether it had been I or someone else who had visited them I cannot say. Unfortunately, any images of people, had there ever been any, had been omitted or removed. (There were several empty slots throughout the book, I noted.) Neither were there any names, dates, or captions of any sort. Yet they must have held some special significance to me, or to whomever it was who had placed them there. They were all of them narrow glimpses into a mysterious past which I have ever since been seeking to unravel. If it was I who had taken them, then I must have had an attraction to nature; and though there was an undeniable beauty about them, most, with rare exception, were too random and generalized to be attributable to any specific location, insofar as I have been able to discern. I will try and post them here as well, by and by, in case any of my astute followers can shed more light.

I found nothing else inside the bag: no wallet, no documents, no ID cards; nothing. Just enough of a fortune (as I came to learn) to last for my foreseeable future - which I seem destined to spend trying to repurchase my past.

I returned the items to the leather handbag (excepting the photo album, which I placed on the bedside stand) and lay back down - once again upon the bed without the bloodstained bedsheets.

:: Posting #4 ::

Room Service

.

Later I was reawakened by a knock on the door and a pleasantly muffled voice announcing "*Housekeeping!*" (The door was on the far side of the suite, opposite my oceanfront window.) When I failed to respond, an attractive, middle-aged Hispanic lady came waltzing in, through the small sitting and dining area and down the narrow corridor which divided the entrance to my bathroom on the one side from my small kitchenette upon the other. She pulled up short as she entered the main guestroom and her eyes fell first upon the pile of bloody sheets on the empty bed, and then on my own bedraggled self upon the other.

"Are you okay, señor?" she asked - her tone and expression clearly indicating that she didn't think so

Wishing to alleviate her evident distress, I said the first thing that came to mind.

"Yes, I believe I may have had a small nosebleed."

I gave a pronounced and startled twitch as I said so (for it was, in my amnesic state, the first time I had heard my own voice). Which twitch did little, of course, to lend credibility to my claim.

She stared at me with obvious skepticism, but her posture did relax a tiny bit.

"Will you be staying with us another day, señor? And if so, will you be liking some fresh sheets and linens?"

"Yes" seemed the most appropriate response to both her queries, and hence the one I gave her.

She proceeded, somewhat hesitantly, as if to remake the bloodied bed, but I suggested she simply leave the towels and linens on the nightstand and that I'd take care of them myself.

She seemed only too happy to oblige and wished me a good day as she bustled toward the exit.

My conscientious housekeeper must have had some second thoughts or continued misgivings about our brief encounter, however, for not long thereafter came another knock upon my door; this one originating from a well-dressed man bearing the nametag of 'Jacob M., General Manager' upon his suit lapel. I felt instantly envious of this nametag, wishing someone had thought to provide me with one similar. (I should also note that that was not the actual name that he bore, for in most cases I am compelled to change people's names to protect the not-so-innocent – and perhaps to avenge myself in part for not knowing my own.)

By then I had removed the bloody sheets from off the bed and piled them in the corner, along with the similarly sullied towels and washcloths from out the bathroom, but I couldn't very well hide the condition of my face. A second nose appeared to be sprouting from my forehead and dark ringlets had begun to encircle my half-closed eyes. He immediately offered to call for an ambulance or arrange for me to be taken to the hospital. He spoke with a friendly, emphatic accent which was typical, as he liked to boast, of his Indian descent. (The country, not the Native-American culture.) I really didn't want to leave the security of my room, however - which constituted the entirety of my known world back then - so I assured him that I'd be fine; that I just needed some more time to rest.

He replied, in his charmingly chopped syllables, that that would be okay, if I insisted, but that I'd need to pay for another day if I wished to extend my stay. (He did, at least, place my physical well-being ahead of his fiscal concerns.)

Remembering about the money - another of those deep-seated instincts, it would seem - I walked over to the closet and pulled out a pack of hundred-dollar bills from the travel bag, which I proceeded to hand him.

"How much more time will this allow me?" I asked - for I remained genuinely clueless as to its specific value. I only knew that I had a lot of them, that he seemed to be wanting a few, and that I wasn't likely to miss one solitary pack.

This drew a bewildered and suspicious look from "Jacob" - not so unlike the one I had recently given myself in the bathroom mirror. His gaze shifted uncertainly between me and the bundle of bills in his right hand, but whatever moral or ethical dilemma with which he may have been plagued seemed readily resolved: he rifled through the pack of bills, then pocketed the money.

"I'll not ask you where you got these," he said simply (which was mutually convenient, since I couldn't have told him), "but you should be fine till the end of the season, my friend. Meals included, if it brings you happiness. I'll go draw up the paperwork."

I assured him that I was indeed feeling happy with these arrangements, despite all evidence leading to the contrary. I accompanied the statement with a feeble attempt at a smile, which he returned in kind before heading out the door.

And thus, I had made my first friend and rediscovered the power of money, all on the very first day of my new existence.

:: Posting #5 ::

Esmeralda

As it turned out, rest was the very thing I needed most – though I suppose I was lucky not to have slipped into a coma.

By heeding my body's basic instincts, I began slowly to regain my health – in a physical sense, that is, for there was no perceptible change in my mental status. Of course, it didn't hurt that my new best friend - 'Jacob M, General Manager' - procured for me a generous assortment of first aid supplies, while also ensuring that three square meals were delivered to my room each day. (He may have vacillated on his decisions, but he was a man of his word, once he gave it.)

The food was brought to me almost exclusively by my original housekeeper – I'll call her Esmeralda – who worked nine to five nearly eight days per week. I began tipping her with a crisp $100 bill at the end of each day, not realizing there even existed any smaller denominations; but she soon insisted that I only tip her once per week, if I felt compelled to tip her at all. (She confided to me that, while grateful of my generosity, as she had over a dozen hungry souls of her own to feed at home, she was having difficulty explaining to her husband where she was getting all that money, and he'd begun questioning what she was doing in the hotel rooms besides changing the linens.)

Esmeralda was a compassionate and honest soul, and she seemed to have adopted a maternal interest in my well-being from the get-go. She carefully monitored the status of my wounds, for instance, even helping with the dreaded application of medications and dressings – scolding me, every time, for being such a coward when she doused my forehead with the fiery peroxide (of which there was an entire case, thanks to Jake). I screamed each time like a small child - which in a sense I was - but she was nonetheless merciless, using such vast quantities of the accursed liquid that the entire front of my hair turned the color of ripe apricots within a matter of days. To her credit, the wound did heal rather nicely, leaving but a small scar atop my forehead – germs never having had a prayer of gaining a foothold within that sea of peroxide. Of the twelve-count case, there were only two bottles remaining when she declared me healed, and I quickly flushed them down the toilet the moment she left the room.

While exasperated at times by my childishness and naivete (as any mother might be at her recalcitrant toddler), she never questioned my past, nor sought to resolve the source of my cluelessness; and for that alone she was deeply appreciated. But she did display a keen concern for my precarious present, and my equally uncertain future. Thus, it didn't take long for her to notice that I only ever wore the same sullied pair of jeans and the same bloodstained t-shirt, upon which I was forced to admit I didn't own any others.

"What size are you?" she asked me.

When I said I didn't know (had no idea in fact what she meant, though the question did strike me as rather personal), she raised her arms towards the ceiling and exclaimed "Ay Dios mio!" and instructed me to take off my pants.

I was a little discomfited but knew better than to object … there were probably several liquids even more pernicious than peroxide in her housekeeper's arsenal. I peeled off my jeans and handed them over.

She seemed unabashed by the fact that I hadn't any underwear, but simply glanced at the tag on the back of my pants and then tossed them back.

On the following day she returned toting far more plastic bags than it seemed possible for one human to hold. These comprised an entire new wardrobe – including new socks, several t-shirts (all black), three new pairs of Levi's, a nice pair of beach sandals, a fashionable new bathing suit, and, of course, seven pairs of comfy boxers. I thanked her and tried to give her more money, realizing she must have used her own (perhaps spending a good portion of the tips I had given her), but she refused to accept it, enlightening me to the fact that the greed for money was the root of all evil – which only made me more eager to dispose of it.

(Jacob, by contrast, seemed unencumbered by such superstition or moral conflict, for he never turned down a tip when paying me a visit. But nor did he make a nuisance of himself, and he too respected my privacy.)

And so it went, throughout those early days of my anonymous existence.

:: Posting #6 ::

Secrets of the Sea

Though the outer me had mostly mended my inner self was another matter, for which time has yet to find a cure.

It took about a month for my bouts of vertigo to subside to the point where I could risk taking brief walks outside my room. The recurring headaches, however, while diminished in their frequency and intensity, have remained with me unto this day, along with the near-total amnesia.

I do recall, with exhilarating clarity, the first day I ventured down to the beach — which was essentially a journey to my front yard. I donned my fashionable swimsuit, a plain black T-shirt, and my sandals (all of which were a perfect fit, thanks to Esmeralda) and headed out towards the sparkling sea.

It was early morning and the gentle sun, which up till then I had only experienced through open drapes, felt especially good against my skin. Simultaneously, a cool breeze conveyed the scents and sounds of the pounding surf which drew me ever towards it, for it seemed as restless and yearning as my own soul. The beach was extraordinarily broad, and that initial trip was a bit tiring; but I had removed my sandals to better feel the sand as it glided over my feet and crept playfully between my toes. I did not stop until I'd reached the water's ever-shifting edge. The waves reached out to anoint my feet with a crisp cold welcome that held me rooted, until both were claimed beneath its grasping sand. A ceremonial, partial burial of sorts, I supposed, as if in gentle warning of the ocean's ultimate power and superiority over feeble man.

Initially I limited myself to wading in those frothy waters but eventually I took to diving and bobbing among the frolicking waves: for while I respected the ocean's immense strength, I held absolutely no fear of it for some reason. Swimming came naturally to me, and all of it felt so familiar - like a tangible link to an unknowable past.

I thoroughly enjoyed those excursions, which developed into a daily ritual – either in the early mornings or late afternoons, and sometimes both. I could stand at length at the water's edge, listening to the wistful sighing and moaning of the mighty surf, which seemed full of secrets it wished to tell…if only I could understand its speech. Its call was occasionally answered by the plaintive crying of the seagulls, who seemed to comprehend what I could not.

I also loved to scan the shore for all those charming little gifts the sea deposited for me each day, and I took to collecting the little stones and shells and bits of coral, wondering how far they might have traveled before landing at my feet. Were there secrets locked within their cores; tales and memories from distant places which none would ever know? In a sense they were symbolic of my own life, and the mysteries now locked inside my head; and they made me happy, and sad, and I loved them all dearly.

But forgive my sentimental reminiscing; it's a relatively recent luxury which I've learned to cherish.

:: Posting #7 ::

My Identity is Revealed

Towards the end of my second month, as the summer crowds began to thin, Jacob stopped by my room on one of his weekly visits with what he termed some bad news. He regretted to inform me that another payment would be coming due if I intended to stay on into the fall – though the daily rates, on the brighter side, would be a bit lower.

To me this didn't appear to be a problem, and I had no idea what the daily rates were regardless; I simply sauntered over to my bounteous supply of cash.

This time my leather bag happened to be sitting atop one of the beds, for I had been going through it a while earlier to make sure I hadn't missed anything important. (A photo ID would have been nice, for instance.) When I opened it, and he saw the size of my stash, his eyes grew wide and his gaze became fixed – which is probably why he missed the pack of bills that I tossed him, which struck him on the left cheek (facial) and fell unheeded to the floor. He never flinched or even blinked.

"That's a great quantity of money to have lying around, my friend," he said with his rhythmic accent. This seemed to concern him a great deal, and he strongly suggested I deposit it into a bank – or perhaps several of them.

I said okay, I'd think about it, and then asked if he wanted to check out my shell collection.

Jacob tended to be of a one-track mind, however, and he wouldn't depart from the mundane subject, asking me if I needed some help opening an account – knowing of my propensity to remain reclusive.

I decided to appease him by accepting his offer, for I really wanted to show him my seashells.

He then asked if I had a driver's license or any form of picture ID; and I told him that, quite tragically, I did not.

"This is a difficult problem, my friend; no bank will give you an account without proper identification."

"Why not just use the name assigned to me on the hotel registry?"

We had had this conversation before (about my moniker), of course, for one of the first clues I had thought to explore was which name had been used when I first checked in – once I realized there existed such a thing as a hotel registry. As it turned out, whoever had signed me in had conveniently been wearing a costume (the Phantom of the Opera … perhaps another clue?). Apparently, they'd been returning from a masquerade or a costume party - which hadn't seemed so unusual for a Saturday night, as the desk attendant had recalled. Whoever it was had also paid for the night in cash before retrieving my unconscious body (I presume) and dumping it into the bed where I eventually awakened. If anyone had witnessed the deed, they would have probably assumed he was merely helping a friend who had over-imbibed at some wild party. Perhaps I had some sort of mask on as well, come to think of it - though I never came across any. This mysterious "phantom" had also used what was obviously a fake name, though ironically apropos:

'John Doe'.

While it excited me at first, this clue had of course led me nowhere; yet Jacob had continued using the name on my receipts (which I never saved).

But returning to the matter at hand:

"No, that name will never do; they'd never believe it. You must somehow get a new one."

"Can you help me with that?" I asked, for the idea of having my own ID, even a fake one, was beginning to sound appealing. Perhaps I could even get myself a corresponding name tag …

Jacob's face constricted and contorted as he appeared to wrestle with some difficult thoughts, but then he smiled at me and said "Yes, I know someone who knows a man who can get you one, but it will cost you a pretty bundle."

I handed him three (including a replacement for the one he'd failed to catch), and he promised to take care of it.

He returned a couple of hours later with a camera and some related gear, snapped a picture of me against a plain green screen, and within a matter of weeks I had an official identity in the form of a New Jersey Driver's License, a social security card, and a matching birth certificate. Had I only known it could be that easy…

Search over, The End.

(Just kidding myself.)

The name on the card read Jonathan D _________ - I'll withhold the last name for now, to keep the IRS off my back. (Although if they do pursue me I'll just confess that this whole story is fictitious and that I don't really own too much money except what was gifted to me by a long-deceased aunt in Tibet which I've already spent and whose name I have already forgotten - and please re-sort those predicates into their proper order and add some punctuation marks; I'm brain-damaged, for God's sakes.) What I can tell you is that it's a distinctively Indian name, the likes of "Basu". Jacob was quite proud of it, of course, and I strongly suspect that he had chosen it himself. When I pointed out that I didn't quite share his distinguishing features, he made a scoffing noise and replied, "Just tell them, with great pride, that you were adopted in India after the great tsunami."

That suited me fine.

And then, at long last, I showed him my shells.

Here, as threatened, is the most recent photograph of yours truly – taken by most recent housekeeper, who also showed me how to upload it.

:: Posting #8 ::

Snapshots

And so it transpired, on the very next day, that the bulk of my money (thanks to Jacob) was hauled for safekeeping to the Bank of America - which sounded the most trustworthy and patriotic of the choices I had been given. The bank manager, also sporting an enviable name tag - we'll label him 'Uncle Scrooge' - seemed only too happy to unburden me of it, though he took his own good time in having it authenticated. He proved quite the generous old soul, however, for in the end he provided me, free of charge - so long as I agreed to keep open my account - a safe deposit box for the storage of my pouch of stones, into which I had added some of my favorite sea-trinkets. I seriously doubt whether he, any more than I, comprehended the true value of the gemstones, however – or of my sea-trinkets either, for that matter.

We were also gifted, Jake and I, with an abundance of coffee and donuts as we waited, and myself with a fancy little pen – thoughtfully engraved with the name of the establishment just in case I should forget where I had left all my money.

I was thankful of Jacob's accompaniment throughout this adventure, for he was far more acquainted with (and hence attentive to) the formalities of the affair; reading carefully over all the paperwork and receipts before allowing me to sign them. He had even made me practice, beforehand, the scripting of my pseudo-signature, with such tedious repetitiveness that when I placed my "John Hancock", so to speak, on the official documents, it had flowed quite naturally. He (Jacob) seemed greatly relieved once my mound of cash had been secured, and I can honestly say I didn't miss it at all – especially once I discovered the power of the little plastic bank card I received in exchange.

My initial purchase with this magical card was a high-tech camera, for I had been enamored by the one which Jacob had used to snap the photo for my fake ID. What compelled me even more to pursue the hobby, however, was the small picture album I have previously mentioned, with which I remained obsessed.

In truth, I did not purchase the camera myself: I handed my card to Jacob, asking him to buy me the best he could find that could still be operated by a brain-damaged dummy such as myself – and to pick up a new one for himself as well, while he was at it (which of course he did). Once he showed me how to use it, there was no stopping me: I began snapping pictures of nearly everything that cast an image. I have multiple pictures of Esmeralda, for instance, wielding every manner of sanitizing liquid and cleaning device known to man – usually in a menacing and hostile manner – each time she caught me with my camera, which was practically every time.

Mostly I enjoyed taking photographs of the seascape, however, which posed with far greater docility: presenting a different face to me with each new day, and sometimes with every passing hour. She's as multifaceted as any precious stone, bending light and color with such dazzling array as the bright sun shifts and the illumination varies, and I've yet to find a more dynamically captivating beauty than that of the Sea – save one, whom I've not yet mentioned.

In consequence of this passionate hobby I have amassed, over time, a comprehensive photographic record of my extensive travels (in search of my own self), but I'll avoid cloying this site with an excess of images. Rather, I'll post a select few from time to time, that you may follow along on my journey, and perhaps recognize something that will aid in my ultimate quest.

Finally, in the ongoing spirit of full disclosure, I must confess to some blatant ignorance which rendered my hobby far more expensive than it need have been – not that I'm exactly renowned for my thriftiness. I've never had much interest in fooling with computers, as they trigger my recurrent headaches - as does the TV. (Which is why I usually have my traveling companion, whom I've yet to introduce and who is the only one I'd entrust them to, transcribe these notes for me onto the computer from my handwritten versions so that all I need to do is post them.) So anyway, when my memory cards were full, I'd simply take them to a processing center and have them print them all out, from which I would cull my favorites and discard all the rest. What I didn't realize, for quite some time, was that the memory cards could be reused, so I purchased a new one every time and tossed the "used" ones into a shoebox - of which I now have three.

The first shoebox has special meaning to me, for it is the one which contained the fancy beach sandals gifted to me by Esmeralda, whom I shall forever regard as my adoptive mother.

Here is one of my very first photographs - an early morning sea in Cape May, New Jersey. (I am no poet, any more than I am a writer, but I couldn't resist attaching a humble verse to this glorious image, for which I hope you will forgive me. I'm a sappy, sentimental young man, as you may have gathered - in case that provides any further clue to my identity.)

The Alchemist

I watched the morning sun ascend
To gild the silver sea
(See how those liquid colors blend
With wondrous alchemy!)
And for a moment it would seem
I saw the hand of God -
Or was it just a waking dream
That made my senses nod
And drift away where angels roam
And spirits wander free
Across this endless, sparkling dome
Upon a golden sea?
If so, I pray I shall not wake
Nor evermore such dreams forsake.

:: Posting #9 ::

The Enchantress

Photography proved the ideal hobby for me in those early days, for it encouraged me to break out of my cocoon; to get out and about a bit more and expand my horizons. It also afforded me the comfort of a lens behind which to hide while wandering amid throngs of people, for I was inordinately shy and socially awkward – still am, to a large degree, and I suspect I have always been so, which is a significant detriment to one who is striving to reconnect with forgotten acquaintances.

In any event, I began exploring the quaint little town into which I had mysteriously emerged, in search of anything familiar – or perhaps, more likely, in search of anyone by whom I might be recognized. And never without that magical device in hand, capable of capturing and freezing time. (The nearest we have to a time machine, when you think about it, though it only ever allows us to travel into the past.)

Cape May is a charming and alluring little town, which has claimed its own special place in my heart: a shining beacon by the sea, back towards which my spirit is ever drawn. (Trust me, I own far more pictures of it than you'd ever care to see, though I can "instant message" you a few if you'd like.) Yet aside from the borderless sea, I encountered no vistas which appeared familiar, nor met any persons who sparked my memory. I saw a few people whom I *wished* I had known, or who made me wish I were less reticent about talking to strangers…

I met Donna at a dockside tavern which served my favorite shrimp and ale. It was a warm and rustic sort of place, made all of wood, where both locals and visitors liked to gather, and hence an excellent locale for me to quietly vegetate and people-watch. The establishment bore a nautical theme, unmistakably, of helms and oars and navigational instruments of every sort, and mounted fish-trophies, and fishing gear, and artful compilations of shells, and authentic, wood-framed photographs of locally historical significance - thus all the ingredients of a place I couldn't help but love. The lighting was subdued, provided by fixtures which hung down from wooden beams, enveloped in shades of multi-colored glass. There was a pleasant mustiness or saltiness about the place, and I would often picture myself inside some ship, sailing away to destinations unknown – or better still, to some familiar yet long-forgotten shore.

My favorite booths were toward the rear of the tavern, in a slightly sunken level, from which I could glimpse the sea through circular, porthole-styled windows. I had a favorite waitress as well – we'll call her Melanie – who became the first person, aside from Jacob and Esmeralda, to recognize and address me by my pseudonym, thus providing me with some sense of identity (albeit a fake one). She was a sweet and lovely young gal, of sun-streaked hair and eyes of smoky green, like emeralds retrieved from a sunken pirates-chest. And best of all, she knew all my dining preferences so that I rarely had to order or wait too long for my food … though I was never in any great hurry. Yet despite her amazing looks and great charm, our interactions never went beyond that of harmless flirtation. (Besides, her boyfriend was the bouncer, and I was in no need of incurring any further head injuries.) She fell somewhere within the range of a professional friend and a caring sister, and like Esmeralda, she seemed to sense my helplessness and tended to look out for me – and I truly don't believe it had anything to do with my exorbitant tips, for she did her best to instruct me that 20%, not 200%, was a suitable gratuity.

But no, lovely as she was, it wasn't Melanie who captured my eye.

There was another young lady whom I began to notice, who stopped in regularly; sitting ever alone in nearly the same location across the room. Dressed always in faded jeans and warm-colored flannel, she managed somehow to simultaneously blend in while contrasting severely with her surroundings. To me, at least, she always stood out, for my gaze kept drifting back to her, like a binnacle compass toward the northern star. (There actually was an old ship's binnacle affixed to one of the walls of the tavern, which is how I learned the term.)

Join me for a moment as I attempt to describe her - but be merciful, for though I can still picture her vividly in my mind's eye, this will be no easy task.

The first feature which captures our attention, as we observe her from an innocuous distance, is the luxuriant abundance of long, wavy, reddish-auburn hair with which she is crowned. Next, if we are fortunate enough to draw nearer, we may catch a glimpse of the largest, softest, most beautiful hazel and gold-flecked eyes we could evermore wish to see. And then she stands, alas, to take leave of us (for she is embarrassed by all this attention), and all adjectives fail. She might have been some goddess, you say - as you stare, spellbound, at her receding figure - adorning the prow of a mighty ship; or a mermaid who has lured many a starry-eyed sailor to his willful death … and I'd have to agree with you. Suffice it then for us to say that her form is angelic, her presence seraphic, and her every movement extraordinarily alluring, for whatever else we might add could not do her proper justice. (I'm afraid, after all, you'll have to finish the masterpiece yourself.)

Certainly, had I been one of the aforementioned sailors, I would have jumped overboard at her faintest calling; but for the longest while she never even noticed me. Her name, which I extracted from Melanie, was Donna – or at least that is the name I have ascribed to her, for the purpose of this narrative. Sadly, I have no photographs of her to share (or I could have spared you the failed description), for though I seldom went about without my camera, I couldn't very well have aimed it at her without appearing to be creepy or extremely rude. There were a few times, inevitably, when she caught me staring, upon which she'd cast me the hint of a smile and then return her attention to the books and notepads with which she was invariably surrounded. In my curiosity and desire to meet her I'd sometimes forget my other woes, which was like a soothing balm upon those deeper injuries, though a separate and torturous yearning unto itself.

In the end it was my darling waitress who rescued me.

It was a Friday evening and the place was particularly packed, with limited seating, whereupon Melanie dragged me (literally) over to Donna's booth and asked her if she'd mind sharing it with another loner. My breathing stopped, as did my heart, until I was resurrected by a heavenly voice replying "Sure, I don't mind."

I melted into the seat while she cleared a spot for me at her table.

"Don't mind my mess," she said, "I would have cleaned up a bit, had I known I was getting company."

Her voice was melodic, hypnotic, whereas my own had temporarily abandoned me. She studied me for a moment, with a look of befuddlement or mild amusement, and then tried again.

"I'd ask if you come here often, but I've already noticed that you do."

I smiled imbecilically.

"So, what brings you to this place?" she asked instead.

I coaxed my windpipe into producing some feeble sound.

"Oh, I don't know; just looking for my mother, I suppose."

Not the greatest pick-up line in the history of mankind, I don't imagine – and I probably inferred a broader meaning to her question than what she'd implied.

"Is your mother lost?" she returned, after a perplexed pause and the slightest of grins.

"No, I don't believe so; it's more like *I'm* the one who has lost his way."

"Then maybe *she's* the one who should be searching," she suggested playfully.

"Perhaps she is; I hadn't really thought of it that way."

"Well," she concluded, "I'm afraid I'm not your mother, if that's what you'd been hoping. I *could* be your sister, I suppose, theoretically …"

"I certainly hope not," I said without thinking.

She smiled at this, seeming to catch my unintended drift (though it could have been taken in conflicting ways), and my heart once again fell out of rhythm.

Melanie rescued me then, appearing at our table with my favorite drink – and a similar one for Donna. She winked at me slyly as she deposited our beverages and walked away.

"How did you know what I like to drink?" she asked, suspiciously.

I chose not to reveal my sources but made a mental note to thank Melanie later on, and to double her tip.

After we'd taken a few sips of our preferred beverages (India Pale Ale mine, straight Vodka hers), she asked me "So, are you a photographer, come to solicit a glamourous and high-paying photo-shoot?" - indicating my third eye, which was still strapped diagonally across my chest.

"No, I just like to be prepared, in case I come across something that captures my eye."

"No luck so far tonight then, I take it?" she said, pouting her lower (voluptuous) lip.

"No, I didn't mean it like that at all." (I may have blushed.)

"Just kidding with you," she said, "I know I'm beautiful," and then she smiled again to prove it.

"Meanwhile, if you're not going to take my picture, feel free to stare at me all you like; just don't feel as though I'm ignoring you: I have to keep up with my schoolwork."

She went back to her bookwork and I went back to my people-watching – doing my best *not* to keep staring at her, for she had definitely overtaken the starring role in my new hobby; and it was surprisingly easy to simply sit across from her there, in silence: both of us together and yet each of us alone.

I carried with me a little notebook of my own, as a matter of fact, into which I was prone to jot down my thoughts: about places I visited, people I saw, and sights of which I'd been compelled to take photographs (the combined accumulation of which has aided me significantly in the compilation of this present journal); and I retrieved it from my pocket and began scribbling some more notes – in part to simulate her busyness.

She looked up at me at first, her shapely brows upraised suspiciously (perhaps wondering if I were mocking her), but then grinned dismissively and continued about her work. What she didn't know – and what I wasn't about to tell her - was that I began composing some poems about her extraordinary beauty: doing so right there in front of her, like some clandestine and unsolicited verbal sketch-artist … these in lieu of the photographs I had refrained from taking, which would inevitably have turned out much better. (No worries; I'll spare you the bulk of those syrupy verses - though I reserve the right to include one or two of them throughout the course of my journal, if they seem pertinent.)

If she was curious at all about what I was doing she refrained from asking, just as I withheld from questioning her about her studies. Some of the cryptic titles of her textbooks conveyed the themes of social sciences and criminal justice, and seemed well beyond my ability to grasp, even had I asked. They looked every bit as dry to me as she did sumptuous, yet I was jealous of their ability to hold her attention.

Melanie returned not too long after with some steaming entrees: the house-special shrimp dish for me, and an enormous, fresh-boiled lobster for her. (I was glad to see she was being so generous with my money for a change.) Donna appeared once again delighted - lobster proving to be the single-most effective means, as Melanie knew, of extracting her from her books.

"You needn't have done that," she said to me (which I hadn't), "but if you're trying to woo me, you're definitely on the right track."

I remember very little of our conversation after that, or of the taste of my food: I only recall drowning repeatedly within the irresistible pools of her soft brown eyes, during those brief occasions when she would glance up at me. I suppose I must have eaten, however, for both our plates were eventually depleted, and our mealtime all-too-soon had ended.

I got up to leave shortly afterward, not wishing to overstay my welcome: for, having consumed her crustacean, already Donna's attention had drifted back to her books. (There was no need to await our check, just as there was no need to ask Melanie to put the bill on my tab – 20% gratuity included, which I'd later find a way to augment.)

"Leaving so soon?" Donna asked, looking up at me with what I assumed was feigned sadness.

"I have some things I need to take care of at home," I exaggerated. (My needs being no more pressing than the rinsing of the latest batch of sea trinkets I had gathered along the beach that day, which were still lying on a bath towel on my hotel bed; but I opted to keep those details to myself – both the fact that I collected seashells, and that I lived in a hotel.)

"Wait!" she said, with sudden laughter, "are you sticking me with the bill? If so, that was a very clever move, and one I'll have to remember for future use."

I assured her that I wasn't and wished her good night.

I hadn't proceeded very far when she called out to me again.

"Hey, you never told me your name; I don't usually accept dinner from a total stranger, you know."

I returned her smile.

"Just call me John," I said.

"Okay; good-night then, John-boy. Now, aren't you supposed to ask me for my name as well - and maybe even my phone number, just in case we never meet again?"

"I already have your name," I responded, "and I know exactly where to find you."

Which *had* to have sounded completely creepy, in retrospect; but she merely responded with her amused (if somewhat bemused) look again before I turned and walked away.

Later I discovered that Melanie had had a single red rose delivered to her table on my behalf, along with a slice of cherry-covered cheesecake. I still have no idea where she obtained the flower; all I know is that, when I returned to my hotel room that night, I completely forgot about my unrinsed shells. Instead, I collapsed upon my bed and began drifting in and out of a restless sleep, during which I dreamed I had to rescue Donna from a ship of pirates, and we became marooned on some tiny island where we subsisted quite well on love and coconuts. (In an alternate, nightmarish version of this same dream, I was grasped by a giant octopus before making it to our island and got dragged to the bottom of the ocean; pledging, just before I went under, my undying love to Donna while encouraging her to swim on without me – which she did, after blowing me a salty-wet kiss good-bye.)

:: Posting #10 ::

Table for Two

Through my quietly persistent observational skills (which is my euphemistic way of saying that I was truly stalking her) I learned that Donna frequented the tavern without fail every Thursday and Friday afternoon, arriving well before dinner to secure her seat; and I adjusted my schedule accordingly.

She was there, in her regular spot, on the following Thursday, but this time I kept to my usual booth as well, not wanting to appear too bold, or overly eager. (Predatory?)

I followed her example, however, by combining some productivity with my leisure: I brought great stacks of my latest photographs that were still in need of being sorted; my favorites to be placed within my mounting collection of photo albums, and the remainder to be discarded.

She glanced across the room at me a couple of times, I was aware, though I pretended not to notice, and once, when I 'accidentally' made eye contact, she smiled at me (goddess-like) and waved. I returned the gesture (minus the goddessness) and went back to my sorting; feigning, like some adolescent schoolboy, to be mildly disinterested.

Melanie joined me at my table shortly afterward, as she was prone to do during her break times: to check in on me, and to see what sort of sisterly advice I inevitably stood in need of. Considering that she was also, quite obviously, playing the cupid's role, I suspect she may have had some deeper ploy this time in joining me – as perhaps to stir up some latent jealousy within my unassailable love-goddess.

I thanked her for what she had done for me on the previous Friday and handed her a gift I had picked up from a local jeweler. It was an 18-carat diamond tennis bracelet - which had cost me an insignificant fortune, but which I'm certain she presumed to have been fake, or she would have scolded me for it and rejected it.

She started browsing through some of the photographs that were spread across the table; commenting on what a great eye I had for capturing beauty, as she put it. (*If only I possessed the personality for it as well*, I added to myself...) She paused over a picture I had taken of an empty beach house - though it was primarily the background which had caught my eye - and asked how my house-hunting was coming along: for she had recently put me up to looking, after I'd disclosed to her that I was living (quite contentedly) in a posh hotel room. She never asked about the source of my profligate wealth, but she was intent, in an older-sisterly way — as one who had to work hard, just like Esmeralda, for her daily needs - in protecting me from myself, so to speak, and in teaching me to become more frugal. "For the monthly fee you must be paying at your hotel," she had pointed out, "you could easily afford the mortgage to a decent home, which would be a terrific investment rather than a careless waste." Hence my incipient house-hunting hobby, which I'd undertaken half-heartedly, but about which she kept hounding me in a persistently caring way.

"This house looks very nice, for instance," she said, still studying the photograph. Needs a little work, but you can't beat the location. I think you should look up the realtor."

I promised her that I would.

When she got up to go back to work, I noticed that Donna had left her table (for Melanie, while charmingly beautiful in her own way, had been blocking my view of her, which I secretly resented). Donna's books were gone as well, by which I knew she hadn't just gone off to the Wench's Room - the female restroom, as it was labeled, opposite the one for Swains - and I scolded myself for not having walked over to her earlier. (I wondered, too, if she'd noticed the gift I'd presented to my favorite waitress and had mistaken the gesture for something more than had been intended. But it was far too self-indulgent of me to presume such jealousy. - *She*, jealous of *me*? How utterly inconceivable, my superego interjected.)

I went home with a hollow and sunken heart and sought solace, unsuccessfully, in my seashells.

This night, it would appear, the octopus had won.

When I returned to the tavern on the following day (Friday), there was no sign of Donna in any of her usual booths (all of which were far less graciously tenanted), and my heart sank even further.

Melanie brought me a mug of ale, into which I mixed my sorrows. But not long had I been sipping on my bittersweet elixir when my goddess appeared before me like some heavenly vision or magical illusion which I feared might be shattered by my slightest movement; and hence I sat frozen and mute, my beverage halted midway between the table and my lips.

My glorious illusion dumped her books rather brusquely upon my table and plopped herself down without any preamble and said "Well, since we met at my place last time, I thought it only fair that I should crash in on yours. Don't worry, though, I'm not expecting you to buy me my dinner this time."

I tried to hide my elation as I set down my mug, but doubt whether I succeeded. Especially since I had set it down too hard and some of the liquid splashed into my left eye, which I began vigorously to rub.

She handed me a napkin, then leaned over towards me and peered out my circular window.

"Nice view you have from over here, sailor."

She smelled of musky cinnamon, and I was instantly intoxicated.

"Thanks," I responded – my vision half-blurred, but my mind in sudden focus. "Up until this very moment, I thought there couldn't possibly be anything more beautiful than the ocean."

(Redemption.)

I must have caught her off-guard, for this time it was she who blushed, if ever so faintly.

Once again Melanie rescued me from what could have become an awkward moment (for my statement was spontaneous and I hadn't prepared any follow-up), bearing the usual drink for Donna, and a refill for myself. Her diamond bracelet sparkled conspicuously as she set down the glasses, despite the soft lighting.

Donna thanked her and said "Today is lady's night, by the way, so I insist on picking up the tab."

"Sorry," Melanie responded, "but your bill for tonight has already been picked up by an anonymous stranger." (She was much more correct, of course, than she could have possibly realized.) After she'd retreated behind Donna's back, she winked at me and gave me the thumbs-up.

"Wow, you must have a secret admirer," Donna said.

"Perhaps … though it's far more likely that *you* are the one who's being admired."

(Take *that*, Mr. Octopus!)

:: Posting #11 ::

My Beach Bungalow

Though my mind might dwell in there forever, with Donna's virtual memory poised ever before me within our cozy booth, I'm afraid I must leave the enchantment of the tavern for a while for I had some other business to attend to.

I decided to heed Melanie's advice after all and began searching in earnest for a more conventional form of habitation. For though (as I have stated) I was perfectly content within my cozy little hotel room and had more money than I imagined I should ever spend, my wealth nonetheless was neither infinite nor inexhaustible (as I had been urged to realize), and thus I decided a little financial prudence might prove worthwhile over the long-haul. I wasn't sure how far my search for my elusive self would lead me, for instance - certainly no clues had turned up yet in that quaint little town wherein I was still abiding - nor what expense my future travels might ultimately entail. Additionally, it would seem nice to have a more formal, personalized home unto which I could return from time to time.

I won't pretend I was exactly frugal in my ultimate selection, however, for it was not strictly a financial concern which prompted me to look. (Here, at last, the more prevailing truth emerges.) I realized I might want to have Donna over for a visit sometime - to meet with her someplace outside our public tavern, in other words - and to escort her immediately to a hotel room, Melanie assured me, would convey the wrong impression entirely.

I began walking about, taking pictures of all the houses (for sale) which caught my eye, for it was essential to me, above all, that my future home be photogenic. I shared the printed photos with Donna, who had pretty much moved in with me at my booth at the tavern by then - uninvited, but certainly not unwelcomed. Ultimately it was she who chose the winning entry: not knowing I actually meant to buy it, I don't believe, but probably just assuming it was another selection for my endless photo albums, in which she at least pretended to have some interest. ("At least my books are full of pictures," I once teased her, "as opposed to yours, which seem to have far too many words" - which merely induced another charming eyeroll before she dove right back into her sparsely illustrated textbooks.)

It was a beautiful, two-and-a-half-storied, luxuriant dwelling, with a wrap-around terrace on the second level, additional rooms within its many gables, and … but why should I waste your time attempting to describe it, when I can merely attach the very photo which won Donna's eye, and hence my hefty budget? (I'm not that well-versed with those fancy architectural terms, anyhow.) Though I should note that from its elevated terrace and rear-facing dormer windows one could see the ocean, thus fulfilling the second of my two prerequisites, else I never would have considered abandoning the hotel.

Though it was Donna who had inadvertently chosen it, it was Melanie who helped decorate my new home, for I wanted it to seem impeccable before revealing it to my goddess. She (Melanie) proved to have a superior taste for decorating, as a matter of fact, for when she had finished, the place looked every bit as light and lovely as she.

For the principal color of the walls she chose a creamy white, like sunbaked sand, and the windows she adorned with curtains of ocean blue. Most of the floor space had already been finished in real hardwood - like boardwalks traversing my seaside home - and these we merely sanded and polished to restore their original luster. A few of the floors (like those of the kitchen, the dining room, the sunrooms, and the bathrooms) she had us redo with pearl and marble tiling, which glistened with the intricate patterns and iridescence of nacre, or mother of pearl – to employ some of the terms which she taught me as we labored cheerfully together. She even helped me select my furniture, though I had to force her to ignore the price tags, and the pieces she selected matched perfectly with the overall décor and ambiance of the place. Most were of sturdy, cherry-wood framework, with light-colored accents and upholstery.

I marveled at the finished product, and we celebrated together with a 'fancy' take-out meal (pizza and buffalo wings, of course), which we shared at my exquisite new dining room table. We avoided breaking in the fine china from my brand-new cabinet, however, opting instead for paper plates and napkins. The latter of which we barely touched, for we are both of us finger-lickers, as it turns out. (We laughed as we caught one another in the very act.)

Afterward, as she stood at my doorway to say good-night, I gave her a gentle hug and told her "You're wasting your time at the tavern, you know;

you ought to be an interior decorator."

"Oh, I'm not so sure about that," she responded. "I had great fun, but I wouldn't do this for just anyone, you know."

Melanie stood there on the threshold for a moment, with a look that seemed almost wistful or regretful, then leaned up and kissed me on the lips... which was not all that unpleasant, I must admit, though entirely innocent; more like a sibling's show of affection than that of an illicit lover.

I watched from the doorway as she walked to her car, and by the time she turned and waved, a smile had returned to her sunny face.

(My Seaside Mansion)

:: Posting #12 ::

A Change of Fortune

When all was said and done, I spent about a third of my fortune in my effort to preserve it - or roughly a million dollars, give or take a couple of hundred thousand. (My cash was much easier to count now that it showed up as a single, boring number atop my bank statement.)

But I loved my seaside home; and besides, as Melanie assured me, it was a sound investment which was sure to gain value over time. Already, she said, just with the changes and improvements she'd helped me make, it was worth a nice premium over what I'd paid. I had no qualms about all that, however: my only real concern was that there were a couple of empty lots between my house and the sea (for it was on a strip of land that was a bit off the beaten path and had only recently begun to be developed), and hence some other homes were likely to be built, eventually, between my own and the nearby sea. But for now, at least, the only things obstructing my view of the ocean were some natural, sandy embankments and rolling dunes, laced with gently swaying beach grass, and these were visually surmounted from my raised terrace. Similarly, I could view the ocean from the quaint little rooms within the east-facing gables, with their comforting, sloped ceilings and circular windows peering out into the infinite blue horizon.

All in all, I felt I had made a pretty good choice - with Donna's unknowing assistance - and I was pleased with myself.

Then came the difficult part.

I needed to break the news to Esmeralda and to Jacob, to let them know I would be checking out at last from their beloved hotel - for I hadn't officially moved into my new home yet. (Esmeralda still regularly teased me, in fact, when bringing me my morning meal and a fresh set of linens, by inquiring "Will you be checking out this morning, señor, or will you be gracing us with your presence for yet another day?" I don't think she truly expected that I would ever leave, and she seemed pleased to be keeping a motherly eye on me.)

I knew the revelation of my plan would be emotionally difficult: for Esmeralda, because she had virtually adopted me; for Jacob, because of all the cash I gave him; and for myself, because I cherished them both so dearly. So I decided to prepare some special gifts to help ease the parting.

I retrieved the pouch of stones from my safe deposit box and took them to the local jeweler - the same one from whom I'd purchased the diamond bracelet for Melanie, and unto whom therefore I'd already become a valued customer; my intention being for him to help me choose the one most befitting for a necklace.

The jeweler's eyes grew wide as I dumped the sparkling contents of my pouch upon his glass-top counter, and he became increasingly agitated as he examined them with his special tools; for they constituted an impressive variety of types, sizes, clarities, and colors. Most of them appeared far too large and beautiful to be real – which is why the banker had probably assumed them to be costume pieces but was happy to humor me nonetheless with a locked box for my gleaming treasures.

It turned out that every last one of them was not only genuine, but extraordinarily valuable. The select shells and sea-stones he set aside with a puzzled look, but each gemstone elicited a crescendo of *oohs* and *aahs* which he uttered with unrestrained enthusiasm. Fortunately, he was an honest man - we'll christen him Abe - and he provided me with an honest appraisal.

"If these beauties were mine, I'd have them insured for no less than 18 million dollars," he said, staring at me through his binocular magnifiers which made his wondering eyes appear thrice as large as they already were.

That sounded like quite a lot even to me, when I thought of their equivalent in stacks of hundred-dollar bills. (I would have needed about six more leather travel bags ...)

He wound up buying three or four of them on the spot, writing me a merchant's check for two million dollars, and promising me an additional 20% commission on his subsequent profits. He assured me he could easily double the amount he paid for them over time: if not by retailing them to local customers, then by wholesaling them to a larger dealer – perhaps some jeweler from New York, or even Paris, he enthusiastically speculated.

He also helped me select a lovely specimen for my intended necklace (Esmeralda's necklace, that is): it was a gorgeous, uncut emerald, of vivid green and remarkable translucency - from Columbia or South America, he opined. Weighing in at over 13 carats and remarkably free of inclusions (as he attempted to elucidate and I failed to grasp), he projected a retail value on it, once cut and polished, of at least $150,000.

"Well then, cut and polish away, by all means," I encouraged him. "You have an excellent eye for it, I can tell. Two of them, in fact."

I commissioned another gift (for Jacob), as well, to be crafted from some of the jeweler's own specimens, and then returned to the bank to re-secure my pricey treasures and deposit my monstrous check. (The banker gave me a look not too dissimilar from the optically-enhanced jeweler's, and then rewarded me with another pen.)

Within a matter of days honest Abe had finished his expert craftsmanship, having produced a magnificent, 18ct gold necklace unto which the superbly cut emerald was fashionably affixed. He turned out a real beauty of a gift for Jacob as well, which I'll describe a bit later. That one only cost me 22 grand, which made me feel a bit cheap: but it's the thought that counts, as I'd recently heard say.

He didn't even charge me for his hours of labor, for he wanted to retain my business, I am sure.

:: Posting #13 ::

Leaving the Nest

My parting gifts having been procured (and clumsily wrapped) and the bulk of my meager possessions (clothes, photo albums, ocean treasures) having been relocated bit by bit into my future abode, I could find no further excuse to delay my departure. A small step for mankind, yet a giant leap in what had thus far been my rather stationary pseudo-existence…

I presented the news (and my gift) to Esmeralda on a brightly glum Monday morning when she came to my room bearing breakfast burritos and bath towels. At first, she seemed to think I was kidding; but when she saw my good-bye present, she began to cry - at how horribly it was wrapped, I at first assumed, for she didn't even open it. She retreated to her cart and began pelting me with rolls of toilet paper, then came at me with her mop; then dropped the mop and began hugging me, then smacked me upside my head for having kept it a secret, and then held me at arms' length and began crying once again, even as she smiled at me in a proudly congratulatory, lamenting, maternal sort of way.

All in all, she was not quite so emotional as I had been anticipating.

She might have continued with her histrionics indefinitely, however, had I not pointed out that I was only moving about a mile-and-a-half away. I also informed her I'd like her to clean my new home on a weekly basis, had she the time and the interest to do so – for though I knew she cared little about money beyond its evil necessity, I figured she'd probably come to rely on my weekly tips to supplement her modest income, considering the frugal nature of her employer. She repeated her cycle of hugs and tears and smacks (by which I presumed she meant 'yes'), then walked over to the hotel phone aside my bed and called off work for the rest of the day, picked up her gift (still hideously wrapped) and went home, abandoning her disheveled cart in the hallway outside my door.

I had been hoping to see her face when she unwrapped her gift and thus provide her with some cautionary details (such as perhaps she ought not wear it while traversing a dark alleyway), but at least I'd thought to include a note inside the box, which I'd written on hotel stationary. In it, I advised her that the gift was non-returnable and so she shouldn't even try. I further assured her (quite falsely) that I'd fire her as my future cleaning lady should she have the audacity to refuse it, as I'd had it made especially for her and for nobody else as a personal thanks for having tended to me so diligently. Perhaps even saving my life, I further embellished, when I'd been mortally wounded … never mind that I'd developed a severe phobia to peroxide in consequence and would avoid contact with the substance ever again if I could help it. I added that she shouldn't hesitate to sell the necklace should she fall upon hard times, and to merely consider the resultant cash as a more practical gift from me as well – but that she should only negotiate such a sale through "Abe", as I knew he'd offer her a fair price. Finally, with what little space was left at the bottom of the stationary, I wrote down the address to my new place, figuring she'd forget to ask. (Though of course I'd always know where to find her, for aside from this day, I'd never known her to miss work).

Yet despite my wordy attachment I suspected that, once she begrudgingly accepted the necklace as her own, she was unlikely to ever part with it - and woe unto him who might try and remove it from her neck! Her lifeless hand would reach out from her eventual casket, I could imagine, to smack any would-be perpetrators across their astonished faces. She was loyal in her affections, in other words, and fervent about those things by which relationships are symbolized: this being perhaps the most important thing I learned from her, which I have kept with me unto this day. (I still wear a necklace she had previously given me, for instance, bearing a small silver cross; a modest thing, really, intended more as a protective amulet than an embellishment, but no less precious and rare, in my estimate, than the one I'd reciprocated.)

With my leather bag, my camera, and my giftbox for Jacob in hand, I stood near the exit-way for a while after she had left and gazed about the empty room - this place of my strange rebirth - and it was the first time (in my hampered memory) that I experienced a nascent sense of nostalgia; a feeling of sadness and trepidation for having to leave the familiar behind in favor of something new. It was an emotion with which I'd soon become all-too familiar, though it would be tempered by a conflicting, insatiable hunger for exploration and adventure: the driving urge to rediscover the old by seeking out the new, in hopes of locating something familiar in that unreachable horizon.

In any event, having hitched up my travel bag and clutched my room keys, I turned out the lights on this beginning phase of my re-existence, and walked out the door.

I found Jacob in the hotel lobby, busily instructing his chief housekeeper to redistribute Esmeralda's room assignments for the day. He greeted me, when he had finished, with that professional manner which he seldom abandoned, though by now we'd become good friends.

I handed him my keys and told him I was finally checking out, and surprisingly, he hugged me and began crying as well. When he'd recomposed himself (a bit sooner, at least, than had Esmeralda, and with far less hostility), I handed him his present, which he opened without delay.

It was a brand-new name tag, layered in onyx and rimmed with gold, in which his name (his real name) was inscribed in genuine diamond lettering. His sadness was effaced with joy as he fastened it immediately to his lapel, handing me his old one as a souvenir (which I have also kept).

I thanked him for all he had helped me with (such as purchasing me an identity and securing me a bank account), upon which he hugged me again, handed me his business card – to add to the ten identical ones already nesting inside my wallet - and assured me I could call on him any time of the day or night. He even went so far as to write his personal cell-phone number on the back of his latest business card, thus rendering it unique from all the others after all.

When he found out I intended to walk from the hotel to my new home (as I had already done many times before), he insisted on driving me there instead.

He complimented me profusely on my good taste as we drove up to the place but took a raincheck on my offer to come inside for a cup of tea (for I'd procured a special blend of Indian Makaibari for just such an occasion), stating apologetically that he had far too much to tend to back at the hotel. In actual fact, however, I believe he was still too emotional and didn't care to prolong our parting, for his eyes were still watery as he gave me another hug (and another business card) and wished me Godspeed until we should meet again.

I stood watching (squinting) as he drove away in his glistening, metallic, ruby-colored bimmer, which was refracting the sun's rays into a thousand bedazzling points of light. Then I turned away and crossed the threshold alone; officially moving in to my large, empty home.

I snapped this picture of Melanie, as she was heading down to
my private beach after a hard day's work on my new home.
I joined her, of course, and we wound up swimming in our clothes.
I remember her being carried inward by a sudden swell and then lying
there, laughing, upon the gleaming wet sand alongside of me.
I didn't fully appreciate it, then, but she was the greatest treasure
the waves had ever brought me.

:: Posting #14 ::

An Unfilled Vacancy

I struggled to adapt to my new environment, for its spaciousness only accentuated the sense of vacancy. I wound up preferring the snug and angular little rooms within the garrets, making my bedroom of the one with the grandest view of the ocean.

Despite the magnificence of its interior, the feature I loved most about my new home was the second story terrace, from where I could absorb the grandeur of the sea by day, and the splendor of the stars by night. While this scenery helped induce a sense of tranquility deep within me, there remained deeper still a disquietude and a longing that wouldn't be quelled.

I had a house, but I was still a very long way from home…

I looked forward more and more to my meetings with Donna at the tavern, and I relished her company even when she was engrossed in her studies and hence ignoring me by and large. When we did talk, I tended to direct our conversation towards herself: not only because I was deeply interested (I cared about her personality and her mind, you see, and not just her looks - though the latter would have certainly excused any faults I might have uncovered about the former), but also because I had nothing to reveal to her about my own indeterminate past.

I learned she was pursuing, through an accredited online program, a degree in criminology. Her eventual goal, as she once disclosed to me in between mouthfuls of butter-dipped lobster, was to land a job with the FBI, and she was amassing an impressive array of related credits that would render her best qualified to apply. She certainly had the requisite physical attributes and agility for such a job, one could readily perceive, and I could tell, by her determination and self-discipline, that she had the mental drive and capacity to succeed as well – in pretty much anything she might set her mind to, as a matter of fact. When I expressed this to her, in pretty much those same words, she returned my compliment with one of those glorious eyerolls that always gave me goosebumps. (Obviously she had already conquered *me*, as a case in point, without even trying.)

She also very briefly confided to me (over some cherry-covered cheesecake) that her previous relationship had been an extremely abusive one, from which she had disentangled herself only after a great deal of pain and difficulty. Though she spoke minimally and dismissively about it, I couldn't help wondering if this is what had motivated her in her current pursuit, as she sought to empower herself in such a self-determined manner. If so, I could certainly understand it, and I admired her for it; she wasn't one to cower under the label of a victim. Perhaps it also helped explain her guardedness regarding our own relationship, which had not been clearly defined beyond that of a casual friendship and table-sharing arrangement. We remained little more than booth-buddies, insofar as I could tell, though I still cherished our little communions above anything else at the time.

While I never mentioned it, it struck me too that our quests were very similar, though reversed: I was trying to find the past, whereas she was trying to escape it. Well, if opposites attract, I reasoned to myself, perhaps I still had room to hope.

All the while I was working my way up to inviting her to my empty home. I could still sense some distrustfulness on her end, however: fueled in part by the former hurts inflicted on her by my treacherous gender, I wouldn't doubt; but perhaps also by my own – unavoidable - evasiveness whenever she inquired about my background. She seemed particularly skeptical when I admitted to her outright that I'd completely forgotten it; that I'd suffered an accident which had left me with near-total amnesiac. She had merely pursed her lips when I had told her so and said nothing, giving a little shrug of her shoulders before re-immersing herself in her textbooks, in which she seemed to find all those answers which I could never provide.

Still, she never failed to return to my booth on our accustomed evenings, so I felt there had to be some measure of instinctive trust beneath all her skepticism.

And every time, there was a fresh red rose awaiting her on her side of the table, which she would invariably take home with her when she left.

:: Posting #15 ::

Troubled Tides

A full month had gone by since I'd moved into my new home, and I decided to enlist Melanie's aid on how best to extend my invitation to my goddess, which seemed long overdue. I sat in my booth with my favorite waitress on a Wednesday - a day on which Donna never frequented, and so usually neither did I - and together we devised a plan which I thought was a pretty good one.

She suggested I give Donna a formal card inviting her to a house-warming party, assuring me that she (Melanie) would attend as well, along with her beefy boyfriend, to help ease any possible tensions. I liked the idea, to which I added a couple touches of my own: I enclosed, in the card I subsequently selected, the original picture of my house (which she had favored), and a copy of my front door key, as a practical symbol of my trust in her. "A key to my home," I wrote to Donna, "since you've already stolen the one to my heart." As if that weren't bad enough, I also wrote her a sappy love poem. (I could foresee the dashing eyeroll with which she'd receive these sentimental offerings.)

I met her at the tavern on Thursday, as usual, but I had already decided to wait until Friday to spring my invitation, which was for that very Saturday (Melanie had advised me not to give her too much time to think about it and so perhaps chicken out, so I figured 24 hours would be short notice enough.)

She was quieter than usual that evening and even seemed to be feeling morose, but when I mentioned this to her, she simply said she had a lot on her mind. Even the fresh lobster, which I insisted on buying for her every Thursday, failed to raise her spirits all that much. She kept looking at me pensively, tugging at my heartstrings each time she looked away, and I would have squandered half my remaining fortune just to know what she was thinking; what faraway thoughts might be traversing her beautiful mind. But she spoke very little; and still the time passed by too swiftly, as it always did when I was with her.

As she was preparing to leave, I tried to brighten her spirits by telling her I had a special surprise in store for her the following evening, upon which she smiled at me sweetly and somewhat languidly; and then, to my surprise, she leaned down and kissed me upon the lips, ever so softly and so swiftly, then floated away like a heavenly dream. My spirits soared (even as my toes went numb), and I took this to be an auspicious sign. It was the first time she had forgotten to take her rose; but even still, the odds of her accepting my invitation had never appeared brighter, I couldn't help thinking, given this unexpected gesture.

Sadly, however, she was never to receive the card which I had painstakingly prepared, and nor did she ever see my home.

When I returned to the tavern the following evening, with my fresh red rose and my special card in hand, I was surprised to see Melanie sitting at my booth. She smiled at me ruefully as I sat down, then handed me a card that wound up being of an entirely different nature than the one I had prepared.

"Donna stopped by much earlier than usual today," she explained. "She asked me to give this to you before she left."

My heart quickly sank as I opened the envelope, knowing whatever news it contained was unlikely to be good - as Melanie herself had apparently surmised.

Ironically, the face of the card bore the image of a rose. Only it wasn't a bright and fresh one, like the many I had given her, but one that had already begun to wilt – as the one from yesterday, which still sat forlornly upon our table. It was a farewell card, in short, and the gist of her message was that, while she enjoyed my company and all the fine food and drink which I had lavished upon her, she had become frightened by how much she'd begun to care for me, as she was in no way prepared for any sort of commitment. "The longer I wait to do this, the greater the chances of you being hurt, and I really don't want to see that happen." (Her words started blurring even as I read them, and I couldn't imagine any greater pain than that which I'd already begun to feel.) She believed I had some things that still needed sorting, she went on to say, even as she had her own career to pursue. As a matter of fact, she'd just received an offer for an internship within her field of study that she couldn't refuse, though it required her to relocate to a distant town. (The fact that she didn't mention the town's name was a glaring omission unto itself.) Meanwhile she wished me all the best and hoped I would find the clarity in my future which I seemed to be lacking in my past.

"If my heart were a rose," she concluded, "then at least one of its petals will always be yours. The one that says, '*She loves me.*'"

Melanie had remained at my table while I struggled through the note, and I was glad that she had, for I needed her soft warm shoulder upon which to cry.

The octopus, after all, had pulled me under.

I'll include the poem she never got to read,
in the hopes that somehow, somewhere,
in whatever faraway town she may abide,
her beautiful eyes may one day fall upon it,
and she'll be briefly comforted somehow …
before giving it an eyeroll.

Canopy

I close my eyes and clearly see
the symbol of my destiny:
a tender rose who bears the thorn
of life's unjust and heartless scorn!
Beneath her beauty dwells the pain
of many a cold and bitter rain:
And would that I could ever be
her warm and loving canopy
to keep and shield her from all harm,
and breathe her scents, and sense her charm:
For only thus were life complete
and all its bitterness made sweet.

:: Posting #16 ::

Transition

The dissolution of my meetings with Donna, as ill-defined as our relationship may have been, was the final catalyst which set my mind to traveling. My luxurious home felt more vacant and purposeless now than ever before; a stark reflection of the vacuum that persisted within my soul. Not even Melanie stopped by to visit me anymore.

I did stop in at the tavern on three additional occasions, but as it became obvious that Donna in fact would not be returning (as evidenced by the three consecutive roses which were left to wilt upon our table), I could no longer stand being there. During those bleak visits Melanie approached my booth on several occasions - her aching expression a reflection, no doubt, of my own irrepressible sorrow - and it seemed to me she wanted to sit and talk with me each time but refrained from doing so for some reason; and I figured she was simply too busy or perhaps didn't know what to say to ease my suffering.

I received some comfort from Esmeralda, of course, who came by each Sunday without fail to clean my home. There was seldom much dirt or mess to clean, truth be told, but she always acted as though I were living in an absolute pigsty, threatening to bring in crate-loads of peroxide and making such comments as *"Oi, Dios Mio,* you should have warned me; I would have worn my hazmat suit". After she finished expunging the imaginary dust and dirt, she'd insist on cooking me a hot meal, declaring there was scarcely anything left of me but skin and bone. Likewise, I always insisted that she join me, stating I refused to eat alone; and I enjoyed all the care and attention she lavished upon me on those occasions. Once again, she provided the proper balm to try and ease my wounds – though these were far deeper than any amount of peroxide could ever reach.

She sensed on her very first visit after my separation from Donna that something was terribly amiss and didn't let up until she had pried from me the truth.

"You should stay away from white girls," was her subsequent maternal advice. "They're all in love with themselves, and they can never be trusted. What you need is some nice Latino girl who will cook for you and make you fat and give you lots of children. *Dios sabe* you have plenty of rooms to fill in this big old empty dust trap."

She had a way of making me smile through my suffering.

"Is that so? And what about you; do you have any such daughters amongst your hefty brood that you'd be willing to offer me?"

"You're too late - and too early. My oldest are already married and the rest are far too young. You just stay away from my brood!" she warned, though she smiled at me as she said so. "But if you can restrain yourself for a couple more years, who knows?"

"I'll wait, then," I promised her. "But if you keep me waiting too long, I may come after you instead."

"*Madre de Dios!*" she exclaimed, crossing herself and shaking her head as she stood to clear the dishes.

So, Sundays were fairly tolerable, but then came Mondays, and every long and dreary day in between – Thursdays through Saturdays being the worst of them, whereas those had formerly been my favorites.

I enjoyed my walks on my semi-private beach, collecting the consolation gifts which the ocean never failed to bring me, and sitting out on my broad deck in the late afternoons and evenings; but the incessant murmuring of the sea and the shrill cry of the passing seagulls seemed to mimic my loneliness and my sorrow, amplifying a longing (for I knew not what) which had begun brewing deep within even before Donna had abandoned me. Even the stars of heaven, as I sat gazing at them late into the night, shone down mockingly upon me; each one of them like a distant wish that I could nevermore attain.

I had waxed melancholy, in other words.

And even though I had scarcely settled into my new home, I decided the time had come to move on.

:: Posting #17 ::

Luxury On Wheels

I felt instantly at peace with my decision. As charming as it was, there was no longer anything firmly anchoring me to that town: nothing (and no one), at least, that I couldn't revisit from time to time. Still, there were some practical matters to attend to.

First, I needed some mode of transportation more versatile and far-reaching than my own two feet - though these had suited me quite well thus far. Among my sparsely numbered acquaintances, Jacob seemed the best qualified to assist me in that regard, for I had observed first-hand his superb taste in motorized vehicles.

I pulled one of his business cards from my wallet (the one which included his personal cellphone number), for though it was half past nine in the evening, I was eager to set things in motion – not the least of which, myself. I gave him a ring from my house phone (for I've yet to become cellularized), hoping to set up a get-together for later in the week. To my surprise he offered to come over right away, showing up outside my door not more than ten minutes after I'd hung up the phone.

We wound up sharing a pot of that exquisite Indian tea I had previously procured; sitting out on my deck and enjoying a pleasant autumn breeze while listening to the low rumbling of the sea that never slept.

(Oftentimes, while strolling along the beach or sitting alone on my deck, I thought about how far the ocean's voice must have traveled before expressing itself, in heaving sighs, upon the very sands that had been formed through its cumulative expressions.)

The cry of a hungry seagull snapped my mind out of its reverie.

When I told Jacob of my plans to start traveling, he asked me where I meant to go – upon which I realized that, in the same way that I didn't know from whence the tales of the sea had come, any more than I could comprehend the shrill cries of its winged ambassadors, I really had no idea.

"I didn't get that far ahead in my planning," I said. "But wherever I wind up going, I need something reliable to get me there."

"I see. And what sort of budget are we looking at, my friend? What's your maximum price range?"

Again, I was pretty much clueless; but I thought about it in terms of the cost of my home; for whatever I wound up buying, I expected I'd be living in it for a while.

"Oh, I don't know. No more than a million dollars, I suppose."

His cup of tea froze midway to his lips, then he set it back down and then picked it up again and drained it.

"I can probably find you something suitable within that price range," he assured me.

He took me shopping the very next day, and within 48 hours (long enough for my check to clear), an enormous, gleaming new RV - metallic-black with silver flares and lavishly trimmed in a wealth of chrome - was delivered to my doorstep.

The deliverer, who was none other than Jacob himself, climbed down from the driver's seat and handed me the keys.

"Not bad for being $100,000 under budget," he boasted, with a smile as glistening as the excessive chrome on my new vehicle.

I half expected him to have bought a similar one for himself on my account, but this time he wouldn't even accept a tip.

"You've given me far too much already, not the least of which your friendship. Besides, that boat will only get you a few dozen miles per fill-up. Considering it's a hundred-gallon tank, you best hold tight to your wallet, my well-padded friend."

He did accept my offer for another pot of tea, which we drank this time in my spotless, germ-free, air-conditioned dining room. He glanced about my home admiringly and mentioned that I ought to rent the place out if I was meaning to be away for any length of time; both for some extra cashflow - perhaps to offset my fuel costs - and to safeguard my property.

This gave me a brilliantly simple idea, which seemed so obvious I was surprised I hadn't thought of it sooner.

:: Posting #18 ::

A Perfect House Sitter

When Esmeralda stopped over to clean my immaculate home on the following Sunday, she asked me what that monstrous metal beast was doing in my driveway, forcing her to park all the way down by the curb. "Are you carting in busloads of white girls now to check out your new home and its young, eligible, swollen-headed bachelor?"

I gave her a dismissive eyeroll which I'd learned from Donna (though not nearly as disarming, I wouldn't imagine), and asked her to have a seat and rest herself from her long walk up my driveway.

"I need a favor from you – do you like Indian tea?"

"I don't think so," she responded, eyeing me with suspicion.

I set a pot of water on to boil regardless and brought out a plate of left-over kachoris from the refrigerator (compliments of Jacob's wife, whom I'd never met).

"What in Dios' name are those things?" she asked. "I hope you're not trying to cook for yourself nowadays, if these are any example."

"I'm not really sure what they are, but they taste pretty good with tea."

"*Nuestra Senora!* And I didn't even bring my heart pills."

I waited till the tea was ready before springing my proposition - during which time she consumed three of my detestable Kachoris.

"I plan to do some traveling," I began.

"I knew you wouldn't be happy with just a short hop from the nest. You're going far away from me forever, aren't you – probably in search of that gypsy white girl who broke your heart. Go ahead, just tell me now that you're firing me; Dios sabe there's plenty else I ought to be doing."

She was nervously fingering the emerald necklace I had given her, and I could sense her emotional wave was about to become another tsunami. I decided to stem the tide and get right to the point.

"I do intend to travel for a bit, and I can't say just how long I'll be gone – I can only promise you that I'll return, for Cape May will always be my home. The favor I'm asking of you is this: I need someone whom I can trust to keep an eye on my place while I'm away. Would you be willing to move in for a while with your family, and be my house-sitter? Your tribe is large enough, I suspect, to fill up every room in this big empty place, and you and your husband could have the master suite - which I've never even used. All the expenses would be paid, of course, except for the food, and I'd be willing to increase your wages to make up for the inconvenience."

Though I'd been trying to prevent it, she began crying again – only this time, as she subsequently confided, they were tears of gratitude and relief.

I'd had no idea, before she confessed it to me, what sort of squalor she and her family had been enduring. They were a good, productive (Roman Catholic) family of twelve, squeezed into a tiny two-room home. With her husband having been laid off work for a couple of months, they'd fallen behind on their exorbitant rent, and their merciless landlord had just served them a thirty-day eviction notice.

"That settles it, then," I said. "What's unfortunate for you is fortuitous for me, for I plan to embark on my extended journey within a couple of weeks."

I hadn't decided that until that very moment, but it seemed like a reasonable plan.

One thing I knew for sure was that she'd keep the place spotless for however long I was gone; and I had a pretty good feeling that her children, much like myself, would enjoy the crooked little rooms in the garrets, preferring them over all the larger bedrooms.

:: Posting #19 ::

Finding Rami

Looking back on those early days, as I fumbled along in my directionless existence, I realize how fortunate I was with the people I'd initially encountered after my accident – or, if you believe in divine providence, with the people who'd been placed within my path. I could easily have been taken advantage of, in other words; but instead, it seems I met up with just the right persons at just the right times, who were willing to help me rather than exploit my wealth and naivete. Even Jacob, whom I wouldn't describe as 100% honest or without guile, was nonetheless quite dependable and just; and Donna, by whom I had in fact been hurt, had never meant to do so, and had wound up giving me (inadvertently) what motivation I needed to push my life forward…or in my case, 'backwards' might be the better term.

I suppose, then, when it came to key acquaintances, I was due for a change in this pattern of integrity and good fortune.

So, I now had my vehicle and my tentative departure date, but I lacked two comparably important details: a driver, and an itinerary.

I couldn't be sure if I'd ever known how to drive, and a massive, million-dollar RV seemed the wrong vehicle with which to experiment or try and remember, so I decided it best to hire a driver.

In retrospect, I probably should have sought out Jacob's assistance in this matter as well. But I was trying to become more independent, considering that I'd soon be out on the road on my own, so I placed an ad in the local newspaper soliciting a chauffeur. I offered $2500 per week in cash, plus paid meals and lodging, figuring I'd start low and expect to have to raise my offer as the job would require traveling long distances and being away from home for extended periods. To my surprise, however, I was flooded with interested phone calls from the very first day.

One person didn't even bother to call but showed up at my front door bright and early the following morning (it couldn't have been more than an hour after the paper had left the presses), and I was impressed right away with his initiative and drive.

No less impressive was his physical appearance and stature. He was a dark-skinned fellow – as brown as tree bark, truth be told, and looking equally as tough – of Herculean size and musculature. His great round eyes seemed to look all about rather than directly at you, and he seemed disinclined to smile. (All this I couldn't help noticing while he was still standing – or rather towering – upon my welcoming mat.)

He introduced himself as Rami – a nickname, I have always assumed, so I haven't bothered to change it – and informed me he was here to become my driver.

I invited him in, and he had to duck considerably to clear the lintel.

I led him to my dining room table (feeling grateful to Melanie for having selected such sturdy furniture), put on some water for tea, and brought out the remaining kachoris – which were a bit stale, I confess, but not to a degree that couldn't be mended by dunking them in warm tea.

His restless eyes were darting all about my house, I observed, though he sat perfectly still, and I couldn't really say if he was impressed with what he saw, for his impassive expression never changed. It did occur to me that those agile eyes might prove an asset while driving, for there'd be little in his surroundings that would likely escape his notice.

He polished off all six of the remaining kachoris before the pot had even begun to boil, which also impressed me favorably, and as I was filling our fine china teacups, it occurred to me that I had in no way prepared myself to conduct an interview. In the end, I could only think of a single question to ask.

"Do you know how to drive an RV?" (I didn't bother specifying which type, for as observant as he was, I figured he'd probably noticed the sparkling monstrosity gobbling up my driveway.)

He sipped his tea before answering – his hand rock-steady and his pinkie finger daintily uplifted. He then cleared his throat and took a deep breath.

"Yes," he said simply.

I placed my hand on my chin, as if carefully considering his response.

"Well then, I suppose you're hired."

"Where do I sign?" he returned.

"Oh, there's no need for a signature; I'll take you at your word."

He took a couple more sips, and then, after a thoughtful pause:

"Could I have a week's advance on my wages?"

"Sure." (I took this to be his way of testing my reliability, while simultaneously demonstrating his commitment to the job.)

I went up to my tiny bedroom and returned with $2500 in cash, which I handed to him and suggested that he verify. He didn't even dicker about the wages, and nor did he bother counting the bills; but merely pocketed them, trustingly, and said "Thanks." (Unlike me, he wasn't one to over-speak.) "When do I start?" he added unsmilingly.

"One week from today," I decided.

"Okay."

He excused himself, placed his teacup (delicately) inside my sink, and let himself out.

Feeling proud of myself for my swift accomplishment, I poured myself a second cup of tea and went up to my deck.

I heard someone whistling in the distance, and when I walked around to the front side of the deck I saw Rami, strolling away along the shoulder of the road. (Apparently, he didn't even own a car.)

I supposed, in hindsight, I should have asked to see his driver's license, as a sort of minimum prerequisite for the job.

I later discovered I should have done a background check as well, as I'm sure Jacob would have insisted, for it turns out the reason he knew how to drive an RV was because he'd previously stolen one. But I didn't check, so I didn't know, and I spent much of the next three days answering my phone and informing all the other hopeful applicants that the position had been filled, until I finally thought to call the paper and have the week-long ad discontinued. Still my phone rang and rang, late into the night, until at last I unplugged it.

I never doubted for a moment that Rami would return on his agreed-upon start date. "He may be a man of few words," I remember thinking, "but I'll bet you can hang your hat on every single one of them." Which was a saying I'd recently heard but couldn't make much sense of, though it sounded rather savvy.

Ah well, hindsight is twenty-twenty, as I've also heard it said. (A painfully ironic aphorism, in my case, since hindsight is the one thing I most lack.) But at least I'd made a completely independent decision, and of that I remain proud.

:: Posting #20 ::

Travel Money

There was not a lot to attend to during that final week in my new home (what little packing needing to be done was completed by Tuesday), but a couple of things happened of their own accord.

On Wednesday I stopped by the jewelry shop to buy myself a watch, for I'd noticed that Rami sported a shiny gold one which had spurred my envy, and Honest Abe greeted me with great enthusiasm from behind his translucent glass enclosure.

"John! I've been trying to reach you. How come you never answer your phone?"

He informed me he had resold the gemstones which he had earlier bought from me, and he wanted to give me twenty percent of his profits as he had originally promised – which amounted to an additional $250,000 over what he had already paid me. (A couple of years' worth of Rami's future salary, as I quickly computed, assuming my math skills were still reasonably intact.) He asked if I'd like to sell any more of them on consignment, as he had fetched a much higher price than anticipated on the first ones, offering me a 70/30 split in my favor. I still had a few dozen of them sitting, unappreciated, in my safe deposit box, so I could see no harm in parting with two or three more. I did try and talk him up to a 50/50 split, but he insisted I should accept no less than 65% of the proceeds, and so we had ourselves a verbal accord – which was as good as a signed contract coming from him, as far I was concerned.

I stopped at the bank to cash my quarter-million-dollar check, thinking it might be good to carry a little spending money with me on my upcoming trip, and this time my personal banker awarded me with a custom tote bag along with the customary pen, for it was far too much cash for me to stuff into my pockets. While I was at it, I withdrew three more of my gemstones, of variable size and color (leaving a residual of 35, if I counted correctly), and dropped them off with trusty Abe.

He inspected them once more, mid a constant stream of sighs and susurrations, and then drew me up an appraisal for $400,000 by way of a receipt – though he suspected he would sell them for much more, he informed me, as he had garnered the attention of some pretty notable dealers with the prior specimens. "We're talking about some pretty high-end clientele," he explained, "and competition among wealthy buyers is a marvelous thing."

I was happy to leave all those tedious business details up to him, for I was more interested in shopping. So I bought myself a $22,000 gold watch (even larger than Rami's, I felt confident of, with a face as big as a clock's), then took my bag of loot and went home.

On Thursday evening I stopped in, with trepidation, one last time at my seaside tavern, hoping to say good-bye to Melanie.

I was greeted, at my barren and flowerless booth, by a waitress whom I'd never seen before - for certainly I would have remembered her. She had unnaturally red hair, hedgerows of silver earrings, and was as thoroughly tattooed as your average sailor; yet she was nonetheless rather startlingly attractive. She bestowed a sunny smile upon me which I'm afraid I failed to reciprocate, for my mood was rather somber. When I asked her about Melanie, she said she hadn't been in for a while - had heard, in fact, that she had gotten herself another job.

I limited myself to a single mug of ale and went home, with a burning in my stomach and an aching in my soul.

Friday and Saturday were devoted to plotting out my initial itinerary – the second of the aforementioned missing details – and this, I concede, I arrived upon in a rather nebulous manner (in much the same way, you might reasonably argue, in which I hired my driver). But allow me to explain.

I'd always had vivid dreams, insofar as my abbreviated memory extended – whether induced by my head injury or whether this had always been the case I of course cannot say – and I had recently become obsessed with an exciting notion: perhaps those dreams were affording me a glimpse into my murky past; perhaps my subconscious mind could partially achieve what my conscious mind could not. I clung to that feasibility to the extent that I looked forward to bedtime, and even fell into the habit of napping in the early afternoons. (Every worthy dream requires a certain amount of self-sacrifice, after all.)

Of late it was a large, open body of water that repeatedly infiltrated my sleep. This would not have seemed in any way unusual since I was constantly near the ocean, but for some strangely specific details: I kept finding myself in the back of a roomy old car traversing an elongated bridge, with expanses of water on either side that seemed far too vast to be anything but the sea, an open bay, or at the very least an enormous lake. I struggled, both in the dreams and afterwards, to distinguish the driver and his companion in the front seat, for they were but featureless silhouettes who never looked back. Sometimes they spoke to one another in low whispers, and the most I could ever discern (whether awake or yet sleeping) was that they were a man and a woman - *my parents?* - and I kept hoping the next dream would provide more clarity.

With this recurring dream in mind, I spent much of the next two days doing some research at the local library. I pored through countless travel magazines in search of something comparable to the scenery I had dreamt, and I wound up settling on the Florida Keys, with its 42 interconnecting bridges (one of them an astonishing seven miles long), as my initial "port of call".

As a reinforcement to this general notion, one of the photographs in my original album was of a slightly hazed and blurred expanse of water (presumably the ocean), which might well have been taken from a car window while traversing that very same bridge of my dreams. The soft interplay of colors, haze and broken sunlight made the picture seem downright dreamy, in fact, which is probably why it had been included in the album.

And so the final piece of the puzzle, or hopefully the first piece to my puzzling past, had been set in place.

:: Posting #21 ::

Last Supper

On the final Sunday before my scheduled departure (which I had set for the very next day, presuming Rami showed up for his prepaid duty as pledged), Esmeralda surprised me by bringing along her entire family for cleaning day and throwing me a farewell party - a feat which had required two separate trips in their old jalopy.

Her husband was a meek and quiet man whom I immediately liked (and whom I'll dub Quasimodo, both for his silent demeanor and for consistency of theme), who nonetheless couldn't stop shaking my hand and thanking me profusely for allowing them this opportunity, though I kept reminding him that it was they who were doing me the favor. His gratitude and astonishment (and his thanking and his handshaking) only increased as I led him on a tour of the sprawling house. Apparently, he shared in his wife's emotional propensity, for his eyes kept tearing up and I feared he might burst out crying at any moment. But he held it together somehow; nearly holding my hand as we walked, for as often as he shook it.

All ten of the children who still lived with them were girls, ranging in ages from six to seventeen, and I learned they had two additional children as well (also daughters), who were grown and married and faithfully producing grandchildren.

Once gathered, she herded them to the dining room table – which, by happy coincidence, provided seating for fourteen – where they sat all prim and proper as she introduced them one by one, and I was charmed by their pleasantry and good manners. They were beautiful young ladies: a garden of flowers; and it was evident that, in whatever ways their parents had to scrimp and save, they made certain their children were lavishly loved, adequately nurtured, and fashionably dressed.

Esmeralda had also brought several bags of groceries and, once the formal introductions had been made, she gave each child a specific task, which they pursued with great energy and glee. Before long an enormous feast had been laid out on my table, even as the aroma of a cake baking in the oven filled the air with added promise.

Afterward, all stuffed to the gills, we went for a walk on the beach like one big happy family. I dug in the sand with the spirited children, and collected sea trinkets, and splashed noisily along the rims of the grasping waves, while Esmeralda and Quasimodo held hands as they sat beneath the dunes, looking on like pleased and prideful parents over their ten beautiful daughters and their incongruent gringo son.

We ended the day sharing cake on the deck – my farewell cake, which the children had happily baked and decorated, and which may well have contained more icing than actual batter. (Perhaps to mask its bittersweetness, I recall thinking.) There was milk for the youngest, and Esmeralda insisted on some good, strong Columbian coffee (instead of tea) for us elders – the age of demarcation between milk and coffee being apparently twelve, to the deep chagrin of over half the children, who nonetheless kept sneaking sips from their older siblings in exchange for extra slivers of cake (from which the icing had inevitably already been licked, as I discovered for myself during one such exchange). I loved watching them, and I adored every last one of them; and by the end of the day I knew each one by name.

They burned some of their inexhaustible energy circumnavigating my deck countless times, playing tag or hide-and-seek, and I noticed how the eldest were consistently mindful and protective of the youngest. When they were summoned inside by Esmeralda to help with the clean-up, they did so without protest, and when they were finished there was scarcely any sign there had ever been a party.

It wound up being one of my happiest, most fulfilling days in Cape May, thanks to Esmeralda and her beautiful family, who took me in as one of their own; and I believe I was even happier than they with my decision to have them stay there.

The only hint of sadness arose when it came time for them to leave. I told them to feel free and stay the night; to consider the place their new home from that very moment. But Esmeralda declined on their behalf, stating she wanted me to have my privacy on my final night – though I was already beginning to dread the impending emptiness.

The children each gave me an energetic, heart-felt hug, as if they'd known me all their lives, and Quasimodo shook my hand protractedly one last time as I handed him a housekey. I had to look to make certain the key was no longer in my hand when he finally let go, for my fingers had gone numb.

He drove the eldest home first, then returned for Esmeralda and the remainder of his meek yet precious family. As the younger girls all circled and clung to their adoring father, Esmeralda stood before me one last time, staring quietly upon me with a wistful smile that was somehow simultaneously joyful and sad.

In lieu of good-bye, I told her the utility bills had all been prepaid for at least a year, and that a twelve-month advance in her wages was likewise tucked away in the nightstand of the master suite (for I knew she'd never accept it from my hand, especially since I'd deliberately overpaid her to an extravagant degree), and then handed her a second copy of the housekey – the one that had originally been intended for Donna.

She was the last to give me a hug, and surprisingly, she did not cry.

I truly believe she wanted my entire memory of that day to be a happy one. If so, she certainly succeeded; for when the door had closed and I stood for a while in the empty foyer - bracing myself against that familiar feeling of being lost and alone which came creeping back - I noticed, in the hallway mirror, that the trace of a smile still clung rebelliously to my reflected image; and I doubted whether even another head injury could have fully expunged my memories of that pleasant day.

I had taken multiple pictures to remember it by, of course, which I later 'developed'; but my eventual favorite was one in which the entire family was grouped together upon the deck, posing against a background of sand and sea and a slate-blue sky, with bright and sunny smiles (many of them cake-smudged) upon their happy faces.

The only thing missing from that picture, I couldn't help noticing (aside from their two eldest daughters), was me.

:: Posting #22 ::

Moving Day

I woke early that Monday morning to an oppressive stillness, as the merry echoes of children's laughter still lingered within my mind: the fading remnants of happy dreams.

Peering out my dormer window I saw splashes of predawn light gilding the clouds over the watery horizon, and I willed myself out of bed and down to the kitchen. Using the equipment and supplies which Esmeralda had left behind and mimicking the technique which she had shown me, I made myself a good strong pot of Columbian coffee – though it's possible I went a little heavy on the magical powder.

I poured myself a cup of the potent potion and went out to my deck, there to enjoy the sunrise over the sleepy ocean. As the morning mist steadily dissolved beneath its mounting strength, I hoped this was a good omen to start my new day – the true beginning of my quest for clarity.

Any moment I expected to hear Rami's happy whistling as he came walking into work. By mid-morning, as no such happy sound ensued, I went back inside to cook us up a hearty breakfast, figuring he'd appreciate something to eat before hitting the road. I wasn't all that concerned about his absence just yet, figuring he'd probably had some last-minute packing to do, and was moving a little slower beneath the added load.

By lunchtime, however, after my eggs had gone rubbery and the bacon had re-congealed within its grease, he still hadn't materialized. No sooner had the cloud of worry begun to form, however, than there came a loud thumping at the front door.

To my surprise, when I responded to the urgent knocking, it wasn't Rami but Melanie who came stumbling through the doorway. She dropped a small suitcase onto the floor and nearly collapsed into my arms – her legs, as it seeemed, no longer willing to support her.

I carried her to my sofa, thinking how light she felt. When I set her down, she maintained her clasp around my shoulders as though fearful of letting go, until I had to gently pry them away so I could take a better look at her.

She was virtually incapable of looking like hell, but on this day, she had drifted pretty close.

It was anger, I believe, that prevented her from crying. Her hands were shaking as she removed her leather jacket, revealing a blouse that was bloodstained and torn, exposing some of the gentle curvature of her breasts, and there were finger-shaped bruises all along her upper arms. There was also some dried blood on the corner of her lip, and when she removed her sunglasses, I noted that her left eye was badly swollen, around which a lurid halo had begun to form.

I groaned in sympathy as I draped her with a throw blanket from off the sofa – one which she had bought me herself.

"Normally he only hits me where no one will see it," she said, "but this time he really lost it."

"Who – you mean your boyfriend?"

"*Ex*-boyfriend," she quickly amended.

It turned out her bouncer had a problem with drinking, and with being too controlling – though he evidently had no control over his anger. I felt outrage over what he had done to her and offered to call the police or take her to the hospital.

"No, don't bother; he's not worth your getting involved. I'm through with him, though: I'm not going back, you can be sure of that. As far as my injuries are concerned, they're really not as bad as they look. I'm pretty resilient, you know, and I heal up quickly."

She hesitated here, taking a few heaving breaths before continuing.

"Would it be too much of an imposition, however, if I stayed with you here for a couple of days? – Just until I can scrounge up the money to head down south. I've no family around here, you see, and no friends I can really trust, aside from you."

I could tell it had weighed hard on her pride to have to ask this, adding humiliation to her injuries; and though her eyes misted up, she still forbade herself to cry. It dawned on me, too, that it may have been because of *me* that she had received some of her beatings.

I was about to explain my own imminent travel plans to her, thinking I might ask her to join me, when there arose another loud pounding on the front door.

Melanie looked up at me in sudden fear.

"What if he followed me? Oh God, I'm such a fool for having dragged you into this mess; now I'm liable to get us both injured, or worse."

I patted her hand reassuringly, though my heart pattered wildly.

I was debating whether to hide her away and answer the door or ignore it and phone the police, when I heard a gruff voice calling out between the poundings.

"Hey, Boss, are you home?"

I let out a sigh of relief and told Melanie everything was fine.

Rami, though in an entirely different way than Melanie, also presented quite a sight when I opened the front door to reveal him. Had the circumstances been slightly different, I might have let out an involuntary chuckle.

Here, beginning at his lofty summit, is a brief synopsis of what I saw:

He was topped with a brown leather cap, in the style of a chauffer's hat, with a gold band above its brim and a bright silver star (larger than a flag's but smaller than a sheriff's) at its center. His upper torso was packed into a brown leather bomber's jacket which was several sizes too small and whose golden teeth had no prayer of ever being zipped, beneath which he sported a light pink dress-shirt and a clashing, cherry-colored tie. His billowing slacks were of navy blue with golden stripes along their outer seams which might easily have once been worn by one of Jacob's bellhops (or perhaps three of them together). Finally, his feet were shod in bright red socks and an immense pair of glistening, golden sneakers which matched his moderately large wristwatch.

"Sorry I'm late, Boss. I had some issues with my laundry."

I suspected he may have washed his red socks with his white dress-shirt, based on my past personal experience.

"It's not a problem, Rami; you're a magnificent sight to behold," I said, waving him inside.

He stooped through the doorway and placed his leather travel-bag aside of Melanie's, not far from the spot where my own bags were sitting and waiting to be loaded, and then stood there like a giant sequoia until I ushered him into the sitting room.

He paused when his darting eyes fell on Melanie, then looked towards me with a mixed expression of astonishment and disgust.

"What have you done to this poor young lady, Boss?"

Melanie smiled despite herself and assured him I hadn't been the culprit.

I wasn't quite sure how to proceed at this point, so I told Rami to have a seat while I brewed us all some tea. (The pot of coffee had gone rather stale at this point and smelled of toxic road tar.)

The conversation - or lack thereof - between my two unacquainted guests must have felt rather awkward, for I could overhear their silence from the kitchen. Melanie later divulged to me however that she felt comforted by Rami's enormous presence, sensing he would have defended her had her ex-boyfriend in fact shown up at that point.

Things seemed to loosen up a bit once I brought in some warm tea and my left-over farewell cake, so I laid out my travel plans: for even Rami, who was to be my professional navigator, had no prior knowledge of our itinerary - though he proved far more interested in the heavily frosted dessert, not even bothering with a fork, and repeatedly licking the extra icing off his massive fingers. (Melanie and I exchanged a quick smile as if to say "Yep, he's one of us.") She appeared taken by surprise at the news of my departure, but it proved easy to convince her to join us on our first road trip, since we were headed in the same direction.

These matters being so simply and succinctly settled, Rami had the RV all packed and ready in no time at all, while I washed the dishes and Melanie changed into one of my soft flannel shirts. By 2 pm, we were backing out of my driveway.

For the second (remembered) time I was abandoning my home, though this time the sense of incipient nostalgia was far less than it had been when I left my hotel room.

I don't believe I even looked back.

:: Posting #23 ::

Our Journey Begins

The RV proved nothing less than a luxury apartment on wheels, with every conceivable (and unpreconceivable) amenity. This, combined with Rami's impeccable driving skills, ensured me that our travels would be cradled in supreme comfort and relaxation, wherever the road may lead us.

Though the vehicle came equipped with a highly sophisticated navigational system, Rami insisted that we stop first at the local Barnes & Noble, where he purchased an immense pile of road maps and travel guides - which he kept spread out, stacked, and pinned up all about the driver's cabin.

"I don't trust those GPS's, Boss: the government can keep tabs on you through those evil devices."

I wasn't all that concerned about the government, but so long as he got us where we wanted to go, I didn't really care what means he chose to guide us. Still, I couldn't resist taunting him a bit.

"This may be just a hunch on my part, Rami, but I'm thinking if you just keep pointing this thing southward, we have a pretty good shot at hitting Florida."

He glanced back at me briefly through bronze-tinted sunglasses, his expression inscrutable.

"Would you like to take over the wheel then, Boss? Cause I'd be happy to sit back there sipping iced tea with your beautiful lady."

"Point well taken, Rami," I responded, raising my cup of tea at him.

The ice cubes clinked against the glass.

"Just keep on driving," I added "you're doing great."

I don't believe he was capable of an eyeroll - and his eyes were invisible regardless - but I thought I detected the trace of a smile at the corner of his lip.

Melanie and I spent most of our time in the spacious living room area, either conversing at the booth-style table (which reminded me of the tavern's), or relaxing in the luxurious reclining seats, where we alternately dozed off or sat gazing at the rolling scenery. Melanie spent more of her time napping than talking, understandably, for she was physically and emotionally drained, but I did learn a little about her mother during those brief intervals when she stayed awake.

Maria, as I'll dub her, had become a single mom at the tender age of 19, and had worked hard and sacrificially throughout all her adult life to support herself and her sole child. Her perseverance and dedication had paid off in the end, as I saw it; for in addition to raising a kind and beautiful daughter, she had also attained success as a real estate agent. She had recently purchased herself a nice little home in Key Largo, in fact - which is where Melanie had agreed to let us take her.

"I feel something of a failure, running back home to mom," she confided, "but she isn't the type to say, 'I told you so'. And I know she'll give me just the right amount of comfort and encouragement so I can put myself back together. God knows she's been stuck with a loser or two herself over the years."

"She sounds like a remarkable woman," I told her. "But I would expect nothing less, having come to know her daughter."

She flashed me an appreciative smile, then leaned across the table and planted a tea-moistened kiss upon my brow.

"Yuck!" I teased her, wiping my forehead. "You best behave yourself, or I'll be telling your mother."

She smiled at me again, which is what I'd been aiming for.

:: Posting #24 ::

Meltdown

We barely made it into Virginia on that first day, and Rami, making good use of his travel guides, found us a pleasantly shaded RV park with all the necessary hook-ups. He even cooked us some thick, juicy burgers on the outside grill (for I'd made good use of my time at the grocery store while he had been buying up the maps at the bookstore) and, memory-loss notwithstanding, I doubted whether I'd ever tasted any better. When I told him as much, he just smiled and said:

"It's no problem, Boss; I *love* cooking on the grill."

So it appeared I'd gotten myself a bonus grill chef, in addition to an expert driver. And he certainly wasn't shy about indulging in his own good cooking.

We sat out for a while at the picnic table after eating, enjoying a late-evening breeze beneath the shade of a beech tree, talking amongst ourselves, and playing cards. Rami was more of a listener than a conversationalist, but he did teach me how to play poker – yet another thing he was remarkably good at, especially when it came to bluffing. It was fortunate we weren't playing for stakes, or Melanie and I would have lost our shirts. Both of which were mine, come to think of it.

"Looks like you've whipped us soundly, Rami. Which means you've won the privilege of piloting our luxury liner again tomorrow."

"You're way too good to me, Boss," he responded, as we headed back inside.

When it came time for us to bed down, I tried persuading Melanie to take the master suite in the rear of the RV: but she would have none of it, favoring the plush living-room sofa instead – arguing that it was plenty big enough for her even without being folded out into a king-sized bed.

Rami was content with the sleeping quarters above the driver's cabin, claiming he was accustomed to sleeping in tight spaces, and in fact he was sound asleep and snoring just moments after he'd drawn the curtains and turned out his light.

Melanie did assent to a nice warm soak in the master bathroom, which featured, unbelievably, a luxurious whirlpool tub.

As she partook of some much-needed pampering, I shed my own outer layers and crawled into my lavish, queen-sized bed, which swallowed me up into its heavenly comfort.

I'm not sure how much time elapsed after that, but like Rami, I must have fallen asleep almost immediately, for my next memory was of being awakened by the subdued sounds of Melanie exiting the bathroom. She was wrapped in a towel and tiptoeing into the bedroom to retrieve her small suitcase, which I'd earlier placed aside the bed, thinking that was where she'd be sleeping.

As the illumination from one of the track-lights fell upon her face, I could tell that she'd finally been crying, having apparently waited until no one would see her.

I startled her when I raised my head, for she'd obviously thought that I'd been sleeping – as indeed I had been, and would have likely remained so, were it not for the fact that I aroused to the slightest noise. (This being a likely result of living alone.)

"Are you okay?" I asked her gently.

That, evidently, was the exact wrong question - or perhaps the precisely correct one - for she turned to me suddenly and reached out to me, accidentally dropping her towel in the process, and crawled into my arms.

I covered her with my sheet and held her tight as she sobbed; fully releasing, at last, her pent-up hurt. She nestled against me as she shivered and wept, and she felt so soft and warm; and I wrestled with my own conflicting bundle of emotions, for she was arousing certain feelings within me that I hadn't even known existed - especially towards her. But I did nothing except hold her close until she'd cried herself to sleep, which wound up being just what she'd needed me to do.

I awoke to soft moonlight seeping in through the curtained windows and the sensation of Melanie's warm body pulling slowly away from me. She grabbed a couple of things from her suitcase and went into the bathroom. When she came back out, she had on a pair of black silk panties and a plain white t-shirt, which clung flatteringly to the contours of her breasts. I regretted, almost resented, that she'd covered herself back up, I'm ashamed to admit.

She had been meaning to fetch some more clothes from her suitcase, but she must have seen something in my eyes: for she climbed back into bed with me instead. Tentatively, she began kissing me on the lips: softly, slowly, tenderly at first, and then with increasing vigor - ignoring, no doubt, all the aches and pains from her various bruises - and I couldn't control the swell of desire that was pressing against her belly. Any traces of her seeming like a sister to me swiftly vanished, as I lost myself to the heat of her passion and slipped into her liquid fire.

:: Posting #25 ::

Aftermath

We must have drifted back into unconsciousness after our blissful meltdown, for I next recall being roused by a soft knocking and Rami's deep voice outside the bedroom door.

"You sleepy-heads ready for some breakfast?" came his muffled call.

We both shot up simultaneously, and Melanie climbed out of bed and headed to the bathroom - wrapping herself in the bedsheet in the process and leaving me there all naked and exposed.

"I'll be right there, Rami, just give me a minute to pull myself together," I said, covering my nakedness with a pillow.

The smell of fresh-fried food hung pleasantly in the air as I threw on some clothes and walked casually to the living room, where a great pile of pancakes and a platterful of bacon had been set on the table.

"Nicely done, Rami" I complimented, admiring his handiwork.

"Thanks, Boss; looks like the kitchen appliances are working just fine. I'll brew us some fresh coffee."

Melanie came out shortly afterward wearing faded jeans and a long-sleeved, pale green blouse which matched her eyes and hid her wounds. The swelling around her left eye had gone down some, but the bruise was darkening. She looked pitifully stunning.

Rami had no comment or reaction to the obvious fact that we'd bedded together, but merely carried on with his self-appointed business. The plates and silverware had all been neatly laid out, and he served us each some coffee, orange juice and fresh toast before sitting down to join us – barely squeezing himself into the side of the booth opposite the one which Melanie and I shared.

We would have seemed a motley assemblage, I am sure, to a casual observer, yet we felt perfectly at ease together, enjoying our meal as if we'd been long-time college roomies. I found too that I had worked up quite an appetite, for I nearly kept pace with Rami's voracious consumption, and Melanie didn't do so badly herself. The food was perfectly prepared and delicious, and there were no leftovers to dispense with when we laid down our forks.

"My compliments to the chef, and the maître d'…and the dishwasher too, come to think of it."

This time Rami's one-sided smile was unmistakable as he wrestled himself out of the booth to clear the dishes – though Melanie and I both helped by loading up the automatic dishwasher.

All in all, it had been a good beginning to our very first road trip.

Our inaugural journey proceeded uneventfully from that point, and Melanie and I maintained our separate sleeping quarters for the rest of the way. We had gained something, without a doubt, during that first night's experience, but we had lost something as well, and our relationship, while essentially unharmed, had become more difficult to define.

I think we both knew it had been wrong. We had both of us been hurting – myself still rebounding from losing Donna – and had sought temporary solace in one another's arms.

And yet, truth be told, it was hard for me to regret it … though many have been the subsequent nights when my oversized bed has felt empty and unfriendly without her in it.

:: Posting #26 ::

Sunset and Sorrow

In Rami's expert hands, we found ourselves rolling into Key Largo by mid-afternoon on a Friday.

Our vigilant and capable navigator located Maria's house with no issues – and without any aid from the GPS, which he had in fact completely disabled. Melanie was duly impressed, for as it was her first time visiting her mother in her new home, she had been unable to provide him with any specific guidance.

It was a modest-sized house, its width being less than the length of our RV, but it was ideally situated alongside the water, upon the upward sweep of a narrow cove. It even boasted its own dock, as I later discovered, though it didn't appear she owned a boat.

Maria greeted us from her front porch with a sunny smile which was the obvious prototype of Melanie's, who led our small procession into her mother's arms. She bestowed just the right amount of affection upon her daughter, avoiding too much fanfare, while gently kissing her bruised eye and welcoming her home as if she were merely stopping by for a holiday meal. She had in fact cooked us up a welcoming feast, to Rami's especial delight, for Melanie had phoned ahead to let her know she'd be getting some company.

Melanie's mother was a slender, pleasantly striking middle-aged woman upon whom time had carved much character without destroying her underlying beauty and gentility. Her light hair was shoulder-length, full, and naturally bleached, and her sea-green eyes sparkled from within a bronzed visage that appeared vibrant and healthy despite a few wrinkles. If she was the future mirror into which her daughter might one day gaze, then Melanie had nothing to dread about growing old.

She had a way of making you feel completely at ease, as if she couldn't imagine anything grander than your company, and the atmosphere at mealtime was just as relaxed as it had been throughout our journey. She even managed to elicit a bit of personal history from Rami, who's background had remained a complete mystery to me — as had my own to him, for that matter. He was reticent to speak about himself, but we did learn that he, like Melanie, had been raised almost exclusively by his mother, and that he'd spent a good deal of time in prison recently for reasons undisclosed — as evidenced by a broad tattoo on his left arm, just beneath his shoulder, which Maria had noticed while he was reaching across the table for some mashed potatoes. It consisted of the italicized word '*Jailbird*', inscribed in large block letters and sandwiched between two dovelike wings. A parting gift from his cellmate, he proudly revealed - intended to commemorate his freedom, I presumed, yet permanently branding him as a former convict. This news was mildly disconcerting, for while he freely admitted it, he didn't care to elaborate on it, either. When Maria broached the subject of his father, it became obvious that this was entirely off-limits, for he shut up like a startled clam. Maria, in her tactful way, did not press him any further, but merely passed him once again the heaping plate of homemade biscuits — which he happily accepted, tilting two or three of them onto his already congested plate.

My own history was even sketchier and far less colorful, for when she politely inquired about it, all I could think of to say was that I'd fallen into a sizeable inheritance and had decided to travel the country to try and find myself — and then I swiped one of the biscuits off Rami's plate and stuffed it whole into my mouth to avoid anymore speaking.

I imagine, at this point, she was simply glad to have her daughter back home alive and relatively unscathed (though little did she know that I had in fact violated her), and she refrained from asking us any more questions.

She told Melanie several times how good it was to see her, and that she could stay with her there for however long she wished, as she cherished the company.

"That is why I insisted upon a home with two bedrooms, hard-nosed realtor that I am, for the extra one will always have your name on it, my beautiful love."

She invited Rami and I to stay as well, despite our dubious pasts, either in her living room or out front in our own RV. I gratefully declined, for I thought it best for us to continue onward: allowing mother and daughter some time for bonding, and for Melanie, some time to begin healing.

Rami insisted on helping Maria with the dishes, and Maria likewise insisted that Melanie and I take a walk together; sensing, perhaps from the look in her daughter's eyes, that we could use a little private time to say good-bye.

We walked around back of the house and sat in a small gazebo facing the water, which was lapping gently against the peers of the dock and the surrounding wooden framework. It was then that I noticed we were on the western side of the key, for the sun was about to set over the ocean: a phenomenon I could not recall having ever witnessed before.

We sat there holding hands as the sun descended in an explosion of fiery colors which the sea slowly doused. It seemed symbolic to me somehow, as if a chapter in both our lives was drawing to its close, and a new one was about to begin – though perhaps, from this point onward, no longer in the same book. For a while we didn't speak, for it seemed there was no need to, as if our thoughts and our feelings were in perfect synchrony.

It was she who finally broke the silence, as the base of the sun encroached upon the rim of the sea.

"I hope you don't feel as though I took advantage of you the other night?" she said with a mischievous grin.

"Funny, I was just about to ask the same thing."

Her smile broadened.

"I wanted you long before you knew you wanted me," she confessed, "but I didn't want to spoil a good thing. Besides, I'm pretty sure your heart still belongs to someone else; someone with whom I could never compete. She'll be lucky if you find her, by the way," she added, with a quick glance below the belt, and then she punched me lightly – though not quite painlessly – in the shoulder. "But if it doesn't work out, or you change your mind, you'll know right where to find me."

It occurred to me then that she probably believed the whole purpose of my travels was to look for Donna, for I had never told her anything different – she still knew as little about me as I knew about Rami – and I decided it best to leave it at that. Besides, it wasn't entirely untrue, for deep down I still hoped my journey would intersect with Donna's again someday. Yet there'd always be a very special place in my heart for Melanie, and I made sure she knew it.

I took her in my arms and we slowly kissed, even as the sun's last sliver disappeared into the water.

That was our true parting – the one I'd remember most fondly – though I hugged her once again when we had all converged on Maria's front porch for our formal farewells. Rami likewise procured a tender hug from our lovely hostess and her indelibly beautiful daughter.

Though confident I'd be seeing them both again (even as they repeatedly made me pledge), it was a bittersweet moment for certain. Yet I had no doubt that Melanie would be well cared-for, and that she was placing herself in the proper hands.

Whatever the future (and if ever I find my past), I'll always feel fortunate to have gotten to know them.

:: Posting #27 ::

Highway Robbery

It was during the next phase of my journey that I learned, once and for all, an invaluable lesson. While of course you cannot judge someone by their outer appearance alone, neither can you do so by their superficial mannerisms. There are hidden depths to people that one may never know; veins that run deep into those unseen wells within their souls, whose waters are sometimes pure and sweet, and sometimes vile and bitter — though most often it is a bittersweet mixture of the two, where the waters, once fresh, have been tainted by merciless time and circumstance.

Neither Rami nor I were any exception to this rule, and I am in no place to judge the quality of someone else's wellsprings; I can only relay what deeds I observed, by which such things tend to become manifest.

We pulled slowly away from Maria's house, while she and her lovely, loving daughter stood waving from the terrace until they drifted from my view…though never from my mind.

Rami, using his elaborate, non-electronic navigational system, had already chosen our destination for the night: another RV campsite, just a few miles away (for we hadn't a lot of daylight left to burn), and the rest of our evening proved lonely and forgettable.

I woke to his cheery call for breakfast, as usual, and though the food smelled rather good, it was saddening to see only two place-settings instead of three, and our meal-time conversation was notably subdued.

"So, where's our next stop, Boss?" asked Rami as we lingered over our coffee.

"Just keep heading southwest, I suppose, until we run out of land. I hope to recognize our location once I see it."

This couldn't have added any clarity to his job, but he remained unperturbed.

"Okay, Boss. I can get us as far south as Key West if you need me to. Beyond that, we'd probably need a boat, because I know from experience these things don't float."

I might have explored that latter statement a bit further; but instead, I was sincerely grateful of his willingness to take direction without question or complaint, and decided, as a show of appreciation, to advance him his weekly wages.

I grabbed my bag of cash from an unlocked cabinet above the fridge and set it on the sofa, where I counted out 25 one-hundred-dollar bills and handed them over. He sat frozen for a moment, napkin in hand, his eyes fixed upon the bag of money. Never before had I seen his eyes remain focused on any one thing for even half so long.

"Holy bat-sack, Boss, where'd you get all that loot?" he finally asked.

"From the bank," I asserted.

His eyes then darted about to the windows and to the doors, as if he expected the FBI or a Swat team to come swooping in at any moment.

"I didn't *steal* it from the bank," I clarified, noting his apprehension, "I merely withdrew it."

"Okay then, Boss," he said, though he still looked nervous, as if I'd just revealed a darker side of myself which he'd never even suspected. *Hopefully he'll grow to trust me in time*, I thought, as he stood up and pocketed his wages – again without counting it, which again I viewed as a promising sign.

We continued southwestward and on across the seven-mile bridge a bit later that morning, and I sat fixed to the window, gazing out over the sun-glazed water, waiting for a sense of déjà vu which never came. *Well, we've come this far*, I thought to myself, *no sense in turning back just yet.*

While cruising through Big Pine Key we came upon a long-haired, scruffy-looking hitchhiker shuffling along the side of the road, appearing severely weather-beaten and withered.

"Pull over, Rami," I said on impulse, "let's give that poor fellow a ride."

He studied him briefly as we breezed on past. "I don't know, Boss; I wouldn't advise it."

"It'll be fine, Rami, you shouldn't be so mistrustful."

"Okay, Boss," he said as he docked our massive land-boat on the gravelly shoulder, "but that dude gives me a bad vibe."

The "dude" picked up his pace once he saw that we'd pulled over, but it still took him a couple of minutes to catch up to us.

"Thanks, dudes," he said as he climbed aboard, unwittingly reciprocating the illustrious title. "I never thought I'd get picked up by such a wicked chariot, but it was worth the try."

I introduced myself and Rami, who acknowledged him with a grunt.

Granted, the young man looked pretty scroungy, like something the cat dragged in then dragged back out in shame; with his straggly, unwashed hair and beard, a tie-dyed T-shirt that looked – and smelled – like it hadn't seen the inside of a washing machine since the primordial day it'd been created, and a pair of filthy, faded jeans that appeared to have survived a vicious attack by a land shark. On his feet he wore nothing aside from the grime and dirt with which they'd become encrusted.

"Pleasure," he said. "The Christian name is Stewart, but most folks just call me Stew. Like the soup," he specified. "You don't happen to be going all the way down to Key West?"

"It's possible," I responded.

"Dude, you're not even sure where you're going? That's rad! Just freewheeling, then; let the spirits take you where they may. I can dig that, man. Mind if I smoke?"

Rami cast me a side-long, murderous look, and I took the cue.

"Actually, I do mind. My driver has a rare breathing disorder," I invented. "Alveolar syphilis," I added for effect – venturing he knew little more about medical terminology than I did.

"Oh, that's bad. No worries then, man, I have some chew."

He produced a wad from a rear pocket and offered me a pinch, which I graciously declined.

Though a little rough about the edges he was extremely friendly, I observed, and it was nice to have some added company again, as he was certainly more talkative than Rami.

He set his leather captain's chair to 'swivel' and spun slowly around, gazing about the lush cruiser, all starry-eyed.

"Holy Shih Tzu, Batman, how much did you have to shell out for this sparkling little oyster?"

"About $850,000."

Rami hung down his head and shook it slowly, I couldn't help noticing.

"Dude, you must be rolling in it!"

"I have enough to get by, I suppose. How about you, Stew, what do you do to make ends meet?"

"You're *seeing* it, man; I'm living off the good land, and off the sweetened, condensed milk of human kindness, such as that which you've extended. Speaking of which, you wouldn't happen to have some chocolate milk in that refrigerator?" he asked, swiveling his chair in that direction.

"Mi frigo es tu frigo," I said, employing some of the Spanish I'd picked up from Esmeralda.

Correctly interpreting this as a 'yes', he hopped up and helped himself, perusing the surrounding drawers and cabinets as well to see what other hidden treasures they might contain.

Meanwhile Rami's imaginary breathing condition began acting up.

"Mind if I have a Tastykake?" asked Stew, unabashed.

"Those are up for grabs as well," I encouraged.

He had also located, in one of the many drawers or cabinets, the remote control to the satellite TV, which I had never even known existed - the remote, that is, though the TV itself had never been turned on. He began flipping through the channels like a gleeful child, responding with exuberance to whatever show he briefly came across; at which point Rami put on his headset and tuned us out entirely.

None too soon, to Rami's apparent liking, we arrived in Key West and pulled into a service station, and Stew decided this was a good enough place to disembark. He thanked us profusely for the ride, shaking my hand with such vigor that a cloud of dust began to form around him, wishing us good favor from the spirits of the island as he snatched my last pack of Tastykakes and took off: unburdened and care-free, with nothing but his tiny knapsack upon his back, which could have held little more than a couple of water-bottles; traveling as lightly as the breeze on a warm summer day, or a half-formed raincloud.

While Rami pumped our fuel – a long and painfully expensive process – I walked into the convenience store to grab some coffee for both he and I and replenish our cupcakes; but when I went to pay, I was told the inside card processor was temporarily down. I informed the clerk I'd be right back; that I just needed to grab some cash.

When I returned to the RV, Rami was nowhere to be seen, either outside or in. Which seemed quite odd, for neither had I seen him entering the store - and he was about as hard to miss as a flatulent giraffe in a crowded elevator.

Oh well, he couldn't have gone too far, I reasoned, so I didn't fret it; but when I opened the cabinet to retrieve some bills, I discovered the entire moneybag had gone missing as well.

The obvious clues added up slowly at first and refused to sink in, but when a full twenty minutes had lapsed and Rami failed to return, the unavoidable facts came crashing down on me.

Not only had I been dispossessed of a substantial (though replaceable) amount of cash, but what was far, far worse, I had lost my expert driver to boot - all in one foul swoop.

Holy bat-scat, Batman.

:: Posting #28 ::

Shoeshine

I was in a real pickle then, parked on my own at a gas pump in an enormous RV which I was completely incapable of driving. I hadn't realized, until that moment, how completely dependent I'd become on a man about whom I'd known so little.

The gas station attendant came waltzing out after a while — I'd say a good twenty minutes had passed since Rami's disappearance — and asked with stern courtesy if I could pull away from the pump to make way for other vehicles. I grasped at a hopeful straw and told him my driver would be right back; that he'd had to take care of an urgent errand. (I was going to throw in something about his alveolar syphilis but thought that might be stretching it a bit in this case.)

Lo and behold, no sooner had I spoken it than my wishful confabulation came true: for what, just past the attendant's shoulder, to my wondering eyes should appear, but Rami himself trundling back in our direction; my bag of loot in his one hand, and our bedraggled hitchhiker in the other, looking — the hitchhiker, that is — as if he'd lost an argument with a freight train.

Rami was barely even winded as he stepped up to the fueling island and handed me my bag, and the attendant just stood aside and stared with eyes and mouth agape; he too taken in by the spectacle unfolding.

"What would you like me to do with our sneaky little snitch, Boss?"

As I came to learn from his later account, Stew had evidently lingered nearby and sneaked back into the RV while Rami was pumping gas. He must have been able to smell money - or had perused my cabinets more closely than I had realized - for in no time at all he had grabbed the bag of cash and taken a run for it: no doubt to offer gifts and sacrifices to the generously provisioning spirits of the island. Rami, however, who had maintained his suspicions about our free-spirited wanderer from the outset, had instinctively come back around from the driver's side and had seen him taking off, and had paused just long enough to turn off the pump before sprinting on after him. It had taken him a while to catch up to him, for Stew proved quite fleet-footed and nimble; but Rami persevered and outlasted him and had taken him down with ease - flipping him into an open dumpster behind a Winn-Dixie, from whence he had dragged him back and deposited him at my feet.

Our involuntary dumpster-diver looked every bit as bad as he smelled, as Rami stood there clutching him by the scruff of his tie-dye, whereby his scrawny midriff had become exposed, and his sparse ribcage keenly defined. Many new hues had been added to his shirt of many colors, and I couldn't differentiate between the ones which were slime, grime, blood, or just rotting refuse, and the various others that had already been there.

"I don't know, Rami, he looks as though he may have learned his lesson. Perhaps you ought to let him go."

Stew nodded his agreement with what vigor he could muster, while the attendant, clunky cell phone in hand and his finger hovering above the keypad, informed us he had 911 on speed-dial, in case we'd like to involve the authorities. A small crowd of would-be gas pumpers had also gathered around, their former impatience displaced by curiosity and amusement.

"You sure about that, Boss?"

Stew and I nodded our heads in perfect synchrony.

"Okay, but if we're not going to turn him in, I think we ought to make him turn out his pockets, at least."

Stew did so with cautious reluctance (for he had no other option), and some sizable wads of cash dropped to the pavement, which the attendant, ever eager to assist, began retrieving for us.

"Hey, wait a minute," protested Stew, "that's *my* money; I already had it before stealing yours!"

Rami cast a disbelieving look in my direction.

"Let him have it, Rami; to tell the truth, I can't be sure how much was in the bag to begin with, because I never counted it."

Begrudgingly, Rami released his prisoner, who nearly fell (like his wads of money) to the pavement before regaining his footing. He appeared eager to chase after some of the loose bills that had begun blowing away, to the scattering delight of our innocent bystanders, but he walked up to me first, and for a moment I thought he was going to shake my hand and express his gratitude once again. Instead, he merely spit on my shoe and took off.

"Okay, nothing more to see here," said the attendant to a crowd that had already begun to disperse, drifting in whatever direction the capricious wind with its floating cash might lead them, in inadvertent homage to Stew's free-spiritedness.

Rami handed me a paper towel from the dispenser so I could wipe off my shoe, then walked back around to finish pumping our gas.

The worth of recovering most of my spending-money?

Negligible.

The value of having Rami back?

Priceless.

:: Posting #29 ::

Sunken Treasure

With that episode happily resolved and invaluable lessons indelibly learned, it remained for me to determine our next move…which wound up being to remain stationary.

We found a suitable campsite for our gleaming behemoth within easy strolling distance of the island's edge and spent several days exploring the bustling little town of Key West: sight-seeing, really, and people-watching, like a couple of annoying tourists. There was much to take in, for it was a well-diversified coastal community, combining much of the old and the new: from its historical sites and conch-style homes to its ritzier resorts and endless quaint shops and eateries along the docks and quays. The island gods had shown the place much favor, in other words, as Stew would surely attest – though we doubted if the poor fellow had remained anywhere in the vicinity following our unfavorable encounter.

I did learn to keep the RV locked whenever we were away, just in case, and Rami had a burglar alarm system installed as further measure - though it wasn't really connected to anything and did little more than make a hideous shrieking noise every time (as occurred without fail) I forgot to disarm it.

While we took interest in what we saw and great pleasure in the local cuisine, I experienced nothing at first that sparked familiarity, with one notable exception: Key Lime pie, which was mouth-wateringly stupendous, and I was certain I had relished the taste sometime before … so perhaps I was still on track after all, I inferred.

Not long thereafter my (pie-induced?) dreams began to shift, or perhaps to grow more specific, focusing not so much on the shoreline but the water itself, surrounded by nothing … and beneath the water, something glistening; something of great value or significance which I needed to retrieve. Inevitably, in this new recurring dream, I would dive down close to the object; but my dreaming eyes could not perceive what my immaterial hands reached out to grasp.

Though there were no photos in my album to corroborate it, I became more and more convinced that there was something sunken in the surrounding sea which would lend clarity to my quest. Granted it seemed the aquatic equivalent to a needle in a haystack, but at least the ocean wasn't exceedingly deep around this island chain, and it seemed worth a shot – since I had little to lose, and nothing else to go on.

This new whim of mine, of course, led to another sizable "investment": I bought a yacht, which seemed only logical if we were going to explore the water, and because – well, why not? I could hear Melanie's voice in my head reasoning against it, but she lost the argument in absentia, and, being left to my own devices, I may have gone a little overboard, so to speak. I bought a mid-sized luxury model with a below deck cabin suitable for overnight and multi-day cruising, equipped with many bells and whistles which I would never even learn how to operate.

Rami agreed – somewhat reluctantly, I couldn't help noticing – to participate in my new adventure, expanding his role from RV driver, grill master and bodyguard to nautical captain as well.

Our purchase included free delivery to our marina of choice and unlimited operating lessons to boot. Rami mastered the craft in no time at all, by which I was unsurprised, and so our careers as swarthy seamen began with minimal delay.

Diving, much like swimming, came naturally to me – it never even occurred to me that I might not have known how, which could have proven rather embarrassing. With the addition of some fins, goggles, and a snorkel, I was ready to explore the dazzling depths of the deep blue sea … or at least the more moderate shallows surrounding the Florida Keys.

Rami preferred to stay on deck; a faithful Captain, overseeing his vessel and watching over his first mate whenever I went snorkeling – and not without good cause, as I soon discovered.

During one of my early snorkeling attempts, I had apparently forgotten – or had never been told – the admonition that one should never swim on a full stomach, for sure enough, jumping in with the added ballast of a hearty seafood dinner capped by two slices of key lime pie bloating my typically svelte form (ignoring, while already in mid-flight, Rami's cautionary protests), I soon developed a nasty leg cramp, and began yammering and flailing alongside the boat like some hydrophobic orangutan. Rami, who thought surely I was drowning or getting mauled by a shark, promptly dove over the side to save me – then began shouting out for help himself: "*Help me, Boss, I can't swim!*" And so the rescuer straightaway became the rescued.

This explained his initial reticence to become my Captain, and I made him always wear a life-vest after that – though it was challenging to find one that properly fit him.

I also acquired a healthy tan during those days – the difference in skin tone between myself and Rami diminishing week by week – and my sun-bleached hair grew rather long, for I had stopped cutting it around the time that Donna left me. I was looking rather different from the clean-cut chap who had left Cape May, that much was certain. I had let my beard grow in as well, and Rami teased that I was beginning to look like Hemmingway.

"Who's that?" I asked him.

"*Was*," he said. "A famous writer who liked to carouse with women from here to Cuba, among other exotic locations."

That didn't sound so bad to the wanderer in me. Curious, I went and bought a couple of his books to read while relaxing onboard and was favorably impressed. I was particularly fond of *The Old Man and the Sea*, for I could identify with the protagonist's love of the ocean and his determination to pursue his passion against all odds. *All he needed was a single person who believed in him,* I thought while reading it. I did hope, however, that at the end of my own quest, I'd be left with more than just a ravished skeleton of my hopes and dreams.

Countless warm and tranquil days were woven together by the rising and setting of the sun over the open waters, with Rami navigating and myself intermittently perusing the sea-bottom around the southern keys. When we weren't boating, we were enjoying the alluring culture and the drinking and dining establishments about town. Periodically we returned to the RV, but on most occasions, we remained in the yacht for two and three-day stretches, supplementing our food stores with whatever fish we caught. I became proficient at spearfishing with a simple, latex-powered device, while Rami was by far the best angler above-decks.

The sense of wonder and weightlessness while gliding through the water – of reverse-gravity, really, for I had to fight against buoyancy to penetrate the watery depths – was yet another thing I felt certain I had experienced before, as I gazed down over the other-worldly seascape; but the *when* and the *where* continued to elude me. And while I added many beautiful specimens to my marine collection, I caught nary a glimpse, for the longest while, of that mysterious sunken object in my dreams.

Still, the search itself was exhilarating – like the old man on his determined quest for that one big fish – and I suppose I could have continued that exotic lifestyle indefinitely, of bronzed mariner, fisherman, and elusive treasure-hunter, were it not for the fact that I one day actually found my treasure.

:: Posting #30 ::

Vegetable Stew

But first I must retrace my steps to relay a couple of notable incidents that occurred on land, which wound up bearing relevance to events at sea.

Just a couple of days prior to purchasing our fancy yacht, Rami and I had been enjoying some breakfast at a wharf side café. While surveying the local newspaper, I came across a chilling article that froze my eye and caused me to spill some scalding hot coffee on Rami's brand-new loafers.

"You having a seizure, Boss?" he asked, no less startled than I.

"No. Sorry about the third-degree burns, Ram, but check out this story" I said, passing him the paper.

It concerned a derelict who had been strolling, northbound, along Route 1, and had been struck rather soundly by a drunken driver who had apparently been meaning to give him a ride but miscalculated his swerve and ran over him instead. The derelict was air-lifted to the Lower Keys Medical Center, where he was being maintained on life-support. They had been unable to identify him, as he'd been carrying nothing but a considerable amount of loose cash, a bottle of water and a pack of Tastykakes (all in his tiny knapsack, which had burst asunder on impact); so they had included a rather graphic photograph in hopes that someone would recognize what remained of him and come forward to participate in the aftermath.

The picture, having been taken post-accident, made him look in even worse shape than what Rami had left him in, but it was unmistakably Stew - as both Rami and I would have known even without the photo.

In a twisted way I felt partly responsible for his happenstance. Perhaps it was the pack of Tastykakes calling out to me, but whatever the case, we wound up paying him a visit in the hospital's critical care unit.

He was on a ventilator, and in traction, and, with all his blood-stained bandages, looking not too unlike a botched attempt at mummification. He never so much as opened his eyes to acknowledge our presence. A nurse and eventually a doctor came by and asked if we were family, and we told them no, that we'd just run into him ourselves, in a manner of speaking, not too long ago. We were able at least to contribute his Christian forename, and his nickname, and they were grateful of that, for perhaps it would help them track down a family member – else the hospital's ethics committee would have to make the call on whether to keep him on life support, as his brain was pretty swollen and it was doubtful he'd ever come out of his coma, we were told. (It seemed safe to assume he had no health insurance, either, which added some financial pressure to their decisions, I am sure.)

I left them my (false) name and the number to our campsite and asked if they could give us a ring before unplugging him, or if there were any unexpected changes in his condition. I even offered to help defer some of the cost of keeping him alive, should all else fail. They were surprised at my philanthropy and grateful of the collateral, assuring me they'd keep in touch. Perhaps I was being a bit over-charitable, but I sympathized with this fellow victim of a debilitating head injury - though he had far more to complain about than I, had he been able to do so. And it didn't seem likely he'd awaken to a mysterious bag of riches.

"Hang in there," I spoke into his one exposed ear before we left, in case anyone was home. "If you pull out of this, I'll buy you a whole case of chocolate cupcakes."

No reaction to that, so I held out little hope.

As a coincidental aside, I should mention that Rami and I took a slight detour to the hospital's cafeteria before heading out, for our emotional encounter had left us hungry; but our appetites vanished when we noticed which 'Soup of the Day' was posted on the small signboard at the cafeteria's entrance.

'Vegetable Stew'.

We opted instead for the nearest Taco Bell.

:: Posting #31 ::

Salted Caramel

The other incident, which occurred sometime later and contrasted significantly with the first, involved a lovely acquaintance I made at a well-known coffee-shop within a well-established bookstore – while purchasing the aforementioned Hemmingways, as a matter of fact. (Rami had deigned to trust me on my own while replenishing our boat supplies.)

She was an exquisite young lady whom I happened to be standing behind at the coffee register, and she had just placed her order for a medium dark-roast and a raspberry scone when she realized she had forgotten her bank card. Cavalier young pirate that I was, I offered to pick up her tab before the order got cancelled. She endeavored to decline, with an embarrassed little grin which was simmering with charm, but I told her she could merely repay me with the pleasure of her company while we drank our coffee.

"I've heard that pick-up line before," she said, "but since I'm not getting any creepy vibes in this case, I suppose there could be no harm in it."

"Good," I responded, "because I'm really only interested in your books. (Of the volumes she was carrying, the one visible to me was about sailing in the Florida Keys.)

She smiled fully at this, by which I already felt over-compensated for the favor, as I placed my order and paid for both - including, against her further protests, her two books.

I was making great strides, I must admit to myself, in my social interactions, even without the aid of my trusty camera, which I'd left in the RV; but she had this way of making it seem easy.

"What name should I call out when your order is ready?" asked the cashier to my far better-looking companion.

"Summer," she responded. (Not her real name either, by the way, but rather close, keeping within the theme of nature.)

As we made our way to one of the small, circular tables and took our seats, I could see why she had to be wary of cheesy pick-up lines, for she was every bit as beautiful as a summer day. She had long, flowing, silken black hair, streaked with golden sunlight, and a richly tanned complexion that was sprinkled with freckles, like cinnamon on warm toast. Her hazel-colored eyes looked oddly familiar - which was always a welcome sensation, in my book.

"Well, would you like to see my books?" she asked, as I tried not to stare. "You have a shared interest in them, after all, since you bought them, so you can borrow them anytime you please."

"As a matter of fact, I would. But only to read the articles, and not because of all the lurid pictures."

Another dazzling smile, and now I was deeply indebted. "I couldn't help noticing you have a nice set of books yourself," she added, with a cute little pursing of her lips and a twinkle in her eye.

We enjoyed an easy, pleasurable conversation over our coffee and scones and our shared library, exploring our mutual interest in Hemmingway and in boating – though mine, in both cases, were in their infancy, compared to hers. She owned a small sailboat, I learned, which she managed on her own, enjoying the sense of freedom and independence it provided. I could tell she was of the type who was completely self-reliant: having learned, perhaps, not to depend on others; and I wondered who had let her down - this seeming to be the common theme among all the lovely young ladies I had met thus far, rendering me increasingly ashamed of my barbaric gender.

Regardless, when I told her of my new-found love of snorkeling, she clued me in on some choice diving locations I hadn't been aware of.

"See there," I told her before we parted ways, "you have already more than repaid my simple favor." I was doing my best to present my gender in a better light, though I was probably no more deserving than any other male.

I rose to leave, and gallantly took her hand and kissed it.

(It tasted like salted caramel.)

"Perhaps we'll meet again someday on the high seas, my Lady."

This won me her best smile, which I tucked away amongst my accumulating store of new and precious memories.

:: Posting #32 ::

Coffin's Patch

A couple of pleasurable months passed by (unbeknownst to Stew) following my encounter with Summer, and Rami and I were out boating, as usual. Checking out, as a matter of fact, one of the prime diving sites she had told me about: a shallow, coral reef about 3 miles south of Duck Key, unenticingly named "Coffins Patch"

The weather was perfect: skies were clear, and visibility below water was outstanding, with the bright sun unveiling the dazzling array of color inherent to the reef and its transitory occupants. Even so, Rami kept calling down to me from the gunwale, like an impetuous nanny, until he captured my attention.

"A storm warning just came across the marine channel, Boss. It's a fast-moving clipper about three hours off, but it's packing some high wind, and the coast guard is advising all small to medium-sized craft return to port."

This explained why most of the other boaters had already vacated and we had the entire place nearly to ourselves. Normally we would heed the warning as well, but I was loath to abandon such perfect conditions. Perhaps this would be my special day, I told myself.

"I'd say we're more on the medium-to-large side of recreational vessels" I suggested to Rami, looking up to him from the bottom of the ladder. "I believe our tub can handle it. What do you think, Captain?"

His restless eyes hopped warily along the darkening horizon. "I'm confident she can" he said, unconfidently.

"Well then, batten down the hatches, I suppose, or whatever it is you're supposed to do, and we'll ride her out. It'll probably blow on past us quickly enough." That said, I dove back beneath the water, which was still glistening underneath a clear blue sky.

About an hour and a half later, however, visibility tanked as overhead skies grew darker, and I returned begrudgingly to the boat.

A veil of grey clouds had overtaken the sky, which paled in comparison to the wall of blackness that was steamrolling in from the east. A gusty wind preceded it, which grew steadily more intense, and the sea that had recently been so calm was soon whipped into a nervous turmoil.

Rami, who had done a much better job than I perusing the boat's operational and safety manuals – considering I had never even looked at them – had already begun the appropriate precautions: securing all windows, hatches, and any loose gear, and making ready the jack lines, safety harnesses, sea anchor, and drogue…or whatever such things were termed, for most seemed completely foreign to me. He then insisted I put on my personal flotation device as well, and I consented with a rebellious sigh. He was going a little overboard in his efforts to prevent us from doing so, I thought, as I surveyed our surroundings lackadaisically.

By this point I took notice that only one other equally stalwart (or similarly foolhardy) boater yet remained in the relatively shallow seas: someone operating a sailboat, who seemed to welcome the gusty winds, and was maneuvering through the increasingly turbulent waters with what appeared to me superb expertise and elation. I immediately thought of Summer, though I couldn't be certain it was her from our distant vantage point.

Certainly, our lone sailor was a lithe female with flowing dark hair – that much was unmistakable – and she seemed to be at one with the wind and the waves and her seaworthy vessel. She paid no mind to our presence, whereas I couldn't keep my eyes off her as she glided and bounced across the rising swells. It was like watching an exotic ballet performance combined with aerobatics and rendered on a liquid stage, and I was thankful we had stayed so as not to have missed it. It occurred to me though that she probably hadn't heard the storm warning, and we decided to head in her direction and try and capture her attention.

We hadn't proceeded very far however before suddenly, like a circus act gone horribly wrong, a terrifying sequence of events took place: her mast appeared to snap in half and her mainsail collapsed, and the entire rigging came swooping down and swept our lovely performer overboard.

She disappeared beneath the churning sea and failed to re-emerge.

Rami, who had been frozen at the helm – equally enthralled by this spectacle-turned-tragedy – sprung to action and maneuvered our yacht towards the scene of the accident, where her sailboat, now capsized, was being swallowed up by the same greedy water that had consumed its mistress. I stripped off my life vest and hurriedly donned my mask and flippers, relying on Rami's eyes to mark the spot where she'd gone under. Once there, he reversed the engine and pointed to the water, and I dove in, knowing he'd keep his eye on the surface in case she floated or fought her way back up.

It was essentially a blind search in the murky depths, and my first four dives proved entirely fruitless, though I fought the burning in my lungs and pressed myself beyond reasonable endurance. I came up gasping for air each time, as I realigned myself under Rami's guidance. To my side, an expanse of sailcloth and rigging clung feebly to the wavering surface, and I checked to make sure she wasn't caught underneath it before frantically diving down a fifth time.

I was beginning to believe I would myself become drowned in my desperate attempt to save her, when a tiny break in the gathering clouds allowed a ray of sunlight to penetrate the gloomy depths, and I spotted a glint of gold on the ocean floor. It was through this that I found her, partially wedged in a crevice beneath the reefs, which had very nearly become her tomb; the glint having come from a golden cross she wore about her neck. She was limp and unresponsive as I grasped her beneath the armpits and pulled her out. I only just managed to drag her to the surface, kicking and flailing and gasping frantically for air as a menacing host of swirling black dots had begun dancing in my field of vision.

Rami alertly tossed us a life preserver, which I affixed hastily around her as my hunger for air subsided and my strength steadily returned. With himself pulling from above and me lifting and pushing from underneath on the ladder we managed to hoist her on deck, where she sprawled and lay like a lifeless mermaid; and Rami, my indispensable Captain, began performing CPR without delay in a vigorous and unrelenting attempt to revive her.

It wasn't until she opened her hazel eyes and began coughing and tugging for air that I knew for certain that it was Summer whom we had rescued.

:: Posting #33 ::

Precious Cargo

With the storm bearing down on us in earnest by then, Rami thought it best if we radioed the coast guard and then stayed put, meeting the squall head-on rather than trying to race it to shore, where it would be perilous to dock regardless. So we carried our injured passenger into the hold, laid her on one of the padded bunks and wrapped her in warm blankets.

I stayed with her there as Rami put out the distress call and returned to the helm, preparing to navigate our vessel through the brunt of the storm while awaiting the arrival of the coast guard.

Summer was shivering and in shock and only partially alert, but she insisted on being propped up, which was probably easier on her breathing as she was still coughing up seawater. A fair amount of blood began seeping through the blankets, and I grabbed our first aid kit and began nursing the various scrapes and cuts she had sustained from the rugged, carnivorous reef. She opened her eyes blearily from time to time, seeming indifferent to the cuts and wounds and the sure sting of the antiseptics (I cringed each time I applied the peroxide), and then suddenly she recognized me and spoke in a hoarse whisper:

"Hey there, buccaneer. You were right about us meeting up at sea someday. You didn't happen to see my sailboat?"

"I'm afraid she's a goner," I told her frankly, "but I believe we salvaged what truly mattered."

She managed a weak smile, then leaned forward and planted a salty kiss upon my lips. It felt cold, but soft, and kindled an unexpected little fire within me.

"A little further up, and to the left," she said; and I remembered I had still been dabbing her with peroxide. "The kiss was in return for the mouth-to-mouth," she added; "Consider it a down-payment." She then closed her eyes and drifted back to sleep, and I knew she had been speaking from within a fog of delirium. Still, I never had the chance to tell her that it was Rami, not I, who had performed the rescue breathing. But oh well, I thought, what she didn't know would never hurt me...

Meanwhile the storm had struck full on, and I suspected it would be a while before any vessel could reach us. Our brave helmsman maneuvered masterfully through the tossing sea, driving prow-first into the angry swells, and though we were jostled around a good bit – giving me an added excuse to wrap my arms tightly around our wounded castaway – I never really felt as though we were in any grave danger.

While it was a far cry from a hurricane or an all-out gale, the squall was certainly more intense than we'd been anticipating. But it passed over us quickly, and in the slowly settling aftermath the coast guard finally appeared, into whose care we transferred our precious cargo.

:: Posting #34 ::

Recovery

We met her at the hospital a few hours later, after we'd managed to safely dock our boat, return to the RV, and change into some dry clothes, and she greeted us wanly from beneath her bleach-white sheets with a constrained smile. She had oxygen tubing running up her nose and an IV dripping into her arm, but other than that she didn't look so bad – quite stunning, really, compared to what I'd previously encountered of hospital patients.

She had sustained a concussion, acquired aspiration pneumonia, and earned a few sutures for some of her reef-inflicted lacerations, she informed us casually, and they had convinced her to stay overnight for observation, against her vehement protests.

"You wouldn't be willing to sort of sneak me out of here, would you?" she asked us sweetly.

"I think you should trust them," I said. "From where I stand, they seem to be doing a pretty good job of putting you back together."

"They're doing okay, I suppose; but I know who it was who truly saved me" she replied – turning her head away, for she'd begun tearing up.

"I better call the nurse, there's something wrong with your IV - I think it's leaking into your eyes."

This brought back a trace of her cherished smile, and I promised we'd return for her the following day.

"I'll cling to that promise, you know. You've always struck me as someone I could trust."

She thanked Rami as well for his bravery as sea captain, and though he shrugged it off and kept glancing around suspiciously at all the high-tech equipment in the room, I knew her words meant a lot to him.

We decided to check in on Stew while we were there, and were startled to find someone else lying in his bed: a toothless old man who greeted us coldly with "Who the hell are you?"

"I don't think this is our man, Boss," Rami noted astutely. The smell of incontinence permeated the room.

We retreated to the nurses' station, where we were informed that Stew had begun breathing on his own and had been moved to a different wing. (We had missed a message from our park manager, evidently.)

We tracked him down to his new room — retracing our steps in the process, for it wound up being on the same floor as Summer's. His eyes were still closed, and he seemed oblivious to our presence. But he did look more human without his breathing tube; and with fewer bandages, he appeared to be slowly emerging from mummification. I gave him a friendly slug on the shoulder, but aside from a brief grimace, he continued lying there vegetatively. I told him to hang tight, and we left.

I waved at Summer as we walked, once again, passed her room.

She had been fidgeting with her IV — no doubt attempting something rebellious — and froze guiltily when she saw us. I paused for a moment outside her doorway and wagged my finger at her before continuing along.

Her voice trailed us down the hallway: "Don't forget where to find me!"

She probably figured we'd gotten lost.

The next day, as promised, we picked her up by cab, our usual mode of localized land transport those days, and took her home.

She was renting a quaint, sand-colored bungalow just a couple of blocks from the bustling docks, within easy walking distance of her workplace and the marina from which she formerly sailed. Her hospital physician had put her on medical leave, advising her to remain primarily on bedrest for a couple of weeks, and providing her with a long list of symptoms with which she should call him or return to the hospital — which she crumpled up as she walked through the door and tossed, with perfect aim, into the kitchen trashcan, on her way to the refrigerator for a beer. I had a strong suspicion that alcohol was on that list of things to avoid, but knew better than to protest, for she had a mind — and a will — of her own.

We did convince her to abstain from work as proscribed, and we visited her often during those days, bringing her groceries and such — which she insisted on paying for, and then forced us to stay while she made us a meal (though this didn't really require a lot of coercion).

"I'm not a complete invalid, you know, contrary to what you might think," she scolded, and though I knew she was mostly teasing, I sensed it must have been tough for her - given her streak of independence - knowing that we'd saved her life. She didn't care to be indebted to anyone; that much was clear.

I tried to reverse this sentiment in her as often as I could without appearing obvious, telling her for instance how fortunate I felt that we had been at just the right place at just the right time, and how saving her life had given my own life a whole new sense of meaning and fulfillment – which was nothing less than the truth. Her countenance momentarily brightened at such statements, but I'm not sure if she fully bought them, for her overall mood remained surly, and still lacking was that radiant smile I'd previously admired.

:: Posting #35 ::

Recompense

Coincidentally, throughout the same period of Summer's convalescence, Stew continued to improve as well, against all the weighted odds that had been stacked against him. About a week after the boating incident, I received a call from the hospital - through Summer, who had allowed me to use her number as an alternative to the unreliable park manager's.

"Sure, he's here; I'll put him on," she answered, and handed me the phone. (I'd been sitting right beside her on the sofa, armed with peroxide, checking to make sure her wounds were healing properly – in a fastidious manner that would have made Esmeralda proud, I am sure.)

"John, here," I lied into the receiver.

An animated nurse proceeded to inform me that our accidental friend had actually opened his eyes and begun to talk. His first request had been for chocolate cupcakes, she noted with amusement.

Rami and I picked up some TastyKakes on our way back in to see him.

His eyes grew wide as we walked in the room, the alarm went off on his telemetry monitor, and he began pounding excitedly on his bedside table (for he couldn't find his call bell), thereby spilling his urinal and accentuating his fist-poundings with splashes of amber. The responding nurse, quickly surveying the distressed scene, thought it best that we leave.

I tossed him his cupcakes - accidentally striking him in his one good eye in the process - and we left without further ado.

I had the taxi driver drop me back off at Summer's – where I knew I'd be better received – while Rami continued on to do some shopping.

It turned out my lovely friend was napping in her room, so I lay quietly on her sofa. I must have dozed off as well; for the next thing I knew she was snuggled up beside me. Wearing not a scrap of clothing, I couldn't help but notice.

When she saw I was awake she leaned over and began kissing me, and the dormant fires of Vesuvius started to churn.

I pulled back, reluctantly, and gazed into those familiar, dreamlike, hazel-colored eyes, which beckoned me inward.

"You really don't owe me anything, you know," I interposed.

"I know, but trust me, this will make me feel better – and probably you as well," she assured me, threading her nimble hand through my sun-bleached hair as she resumed kissing me.

I figured that, since I'd saved her life, she felt she needed to give herself to me, to sort of even out the score. Completely unnecessary, of course - but who was I to interfere with her emotional healing, the darker side of my conscience reasoned. I did feel compelled to come clean with her, though, on the fact that it had been Rami who had performed the CPR.

"Should we wait on him to join us, then?" she teased – or I assumed that she was teasing.

An immediate decision was in order, in any event, ere I was sucked irrecoverably beneath her undertow...

There's a part of me that would like to say that I ceded to her passion, allowing her to take matters into her own hands as she straddled me with her powerful legs, hoisted the mainmast, and sailed me to paradise, and that my memories of Summer would never be the same. But not only would that sound extraordinarily cheesy, it wouldn't be true, and I have sworn myself to perfect candor.

The fact is I knew, in that simmering moment, what had attracted me to Summer in the first place: her exquisite beauty, while still failing to achieve the same exotic plane, had reminded me of Donna. (Her eyes and her smile in particular.) Had I given in to her then I would have, in a sense, been betraying them both. Deep down I knew it just wouldn't be right – remembering, in a flash of mixed emotions, my accidental affair with Melanie, and the awkwardness and guilt that this had engendered. So instead – what truly happened – was that I took her hand (ere it stray into perilous regions) and clasped it against my heart: and I asked her to be still, and just lay with me there for a while. She rested her hand upon my chest, in a state of complete relaxation, and before long I felt the warmth of her silent tears - whether of sadness, relief, or gratitude, I couldn't be certain, but the moment was unbelievably tender and special somehow...until Rami came barging through the door to end it.

"I'm sorry I didn't knock, but my hands were too full," he said, as he juggled a mound of paper bags towards the kitchen. "I hope you kids don't mind, but I picked us up some Chinese food."

We pulled apart from one another, like guilty children being caught in a mischievous act by a parent. Summer wrapped herself in the light blanket beneath which we'd been ensconced as she stood up, then went strolling nonchalantly to her bedroom; her lovely derriere exposing itself partially as she walked.

Rami, who always notices everything, pretended not to notice anything, as he walked right past the sofa and into the kitchen, where he began sorting out our food. By the time he came back out with a couple of heavily laden trays which he set upon the coffee table, I had recomposed myself to a large degree. Summer came back out shortly afterward, dressed in jeans and a checkered blouse; her demeanor casual and cheerful as she spoke.

"Thanks, Rami, you have no idea how famished I was."

All three of us must have been so, it appeared, as we loaded our paper plates with piles of the aromatic grease-laden food; and we enjoyed a casual meal together, right there on Summer's magical sofa.

I noticed, while we ate, that much of the melancholy had dissolved from Summer's face. She at last appeared more content and secure in our company, and as she seemed in the mood to talk, I ventured to prompt her a little about her past – realizing too late that I wouldn't be able to reciprocate in kind should she choose to reverse the query. But apparently my timing was right, for she proved eager to open herself up to us emotionally – even as she had been prepared to do physically just a short while earlier.

:: Posting #36 ::

Painful Recollections

Summer disclosed to us, over a heaping plate of shrimp-fried rice, how both of her biological parents had been irresponsible drug users, and that she and her brother had been long-term victims of abuse by neglect. They had lived in squalor, were poorly fed, and had been left alone for prolonged periods in a home that was barely habitable. Clothed in the same filthy rags for weeks on end, they sometimes shared dry dogfood with a scrawny mutt who took much better care of them than did their patents — until their father one day shot the dog right in front of them, in a fit of rage over the fact that the half-starved creature had accidentally stumbled and spilled his beer. He tossed its bony carcass in the back yard, where Summer and her brother huddled around it, sobbing profusely until their so-called father hollered at them to shut up lest they get the same treatment. Their birth mother, meanwhile, was too strung out on Heroin to react, intervene, or even notice, as her young children — ages seven and eight — began silently digging a shallow grave for their beloved pet and loyal guardian.

Mercifully a new neighbor, who had heard the gunshot, peered over the tall fence, and witnessed this pitiful aftermath. A report was filed — long overdue — with child protective services.

The upshot of it all was that the children were removed from the home, charges were filed against the parents, and Summer and her brother were eventually farmed into separate foster homes — where Summer, for her part, was physically and sexually assaulted repeatedly.

(Here Summer paused to refill her plate, upon which Rami and I both realized we had stopped eating. We took a couple of insipid bites, and then

Summer continued her gut-wrenching tale.)

Things did at last take a happier turn, however. Summer had wound up being placed with the same couple who had taken in her brother, and the close-knit siblings were thankfully reunited. Eventually both were adopted by this elderly but kindly and well-to-do couple, who provided them with the first stable and decent home they had ever known. They even bought them a puppy: an adorable beagle, who never lived up to their former nanny, but who loved and comforted them nonetheless as best she could.

Despite all this, they had difficulty – understandably – adjusting to a society that too often shows so little patience or compassion for the weak and suffering, worrying instead about its own well-being and prosperity.

The years passed by, indifferently, and upon graduating from High School, Summer flitted between jobs and relationships alike, having great difficulty with the concepts of trust and commitment. Her brother, meanwhile, who had graduated a year ahead of her, began following in the precipitous footsteps of his biological parents. He had already begun to delve into alcohol and other soft-core substances while still in school, finding in them some temporarily solace to his lingering pains (as he had confessed to Summer); for there are some wounds that are simply too deep to heal, no matter the intensity and earnestness of the intended cure. Upon graduating from school, he also graduated into harder substances, such as LSD, Heroin, and methamphetamines, to the point where he had begun stealing from his adoptive parents to support his deepening habit - which had begun to fry his brain, even as it dulled his senses. After several failed attempts at getting him help, which had demanded steep emotional and financial outpouring, he had finally run away from them in shame.

(Summer took another pause here, making dessert of a couple of egg rolls while apologizing for rambling on, assuring us her story was approaching its conclusion. We encouraged her to carry on, admiring both her eloquence and her appetite, despite the gruesomeness of her tale.)

About a year had passed by, she continued; a year involving much worry and fear and many fruitless attempts to find him, when Summer received a single letter from her absent brother, in which he disclosed to her his new-found, heavenly haven. He had joined some free-spirited, tent-and-hovel-dwelling community in Tennessee, it appeared – though he had selected different euphemisms to describe it - which sustained itself in part by farming, fishing, and crafting … and who knew what other unlawful, subsidiary activities besides, she couldn't help but imagine, judging by the stark photograph which he'd enclosed. The letter also included a sincere apology to their parents and an invitation for her to join him, but as it didn't seem the sort of place in which she'd care to dwell, she sent him a response pleading for him to return home, assuring him he was still loved and welcome there, and that all had been forgiven, as reaffirmed first-hand

by a separate entry from their parents. But if he even received her letter –
for the return address was simply a post office – he never bothered to
respond, and they decided to let things be for a while, knowing that at least
he was alive and doing somewhat well.

Meanwhile, what the hand of Fate doles out, be it good or bad, she
eventually reclaims, one must presume: for a series of deaths further
overshadowed Summer's bleak subsistence.

First her beagle – though she died of old age, after a long and love-filled
existence - and then her adoptive father, who suffered a fatal heart attack;
induced in part, one might presume, by his fretful worries over his wayward
son. He left her with a substantial fortune and a broken heart; and her
adoptive mother, also dispirited and heartbroken, died but two months
later, rendering Summer an extremely wealthy orphan, having no one with
whom to share her grief, nor her unsolicited riches.

(Here she pushed her empty plate aside, having stashed all that food I
knew not where, and the ending to her sad tale I'll recount in her own
words, to the best of my recollection.)

:: Posting #37 ::

An Unexpected Reunion

"Lost and alone," continued Summer, "I set out to find my brother, that I might have someone with whom to mourn, and to let him know about his portion of the inheritance. I was even prepared to join his free-spirited clan, for better or for worse, if that's what it took to be near him.

"I tracked down his touted commune, beginning at the Post Office that had been listed on his return address, where I received further direction from the locals – though they seemed aware of it as something that ought to be carefully avoided, like a nasty sinkhole. The place indeed looked quite a shambles, like some fall-out shelter that had been hurriedly cobbled together, with people living in squalor and sharing what meager possessions they had – including their drugs and their bed partners, from what I soon gathered. Both children and adults strolled naked or half-naked all about, wearing varying degrees of sorrow and distress on their earthy, weather-beaten faces, and it didn't appear to me as though they were necessarily enjoying this freedom of living off the land, well removed from the materialism and rat-race of civilized society. But perhaps there was more beneath their exposed surfaces than originally met my eye.

"It took me a while, but at last I met someone who knew – or at least remembered – my brother. A woman of indeterminate age, with ratted, yellow hair, a paucity of teeth, and thin and sagging breasts, who told me he was no longer with them; that he had vacated the place just a few weeks prior. 'Three months, at the most,' by her bare estimates. 'He just never really fit in, even with a bunch of misfits like us. He said the dryads – the spirits of the trees, you know – had singled him out for a special mission, telling him to make his exodus and begin a colony of his own. He invited me to come with, I suppose to become the Eve to his Adam, but I couldn't pull myself away from all this security,' she had said, sweeping her dirt-colored arm all about at what appeared to me the remnants of some unnatural disaster.

"'Did he tell you where he was going?' I ventured to ask. She had thought for a moment, which seemed to induce great pain.

"'South,' she said at last, with a single but assertive nod of her head. 'He was headed south.'

"I thanked her for the tip and tipped her for her help, upon which she offered me some weed (extracting it from I knew not where), which I curtly declined. Already I couldn't imagine this was the sort of place I'd fit into any better than had my brother.

"Her clue was rather vague, to say the least, but it was *something*, so I journeyed southward from there with my scrap of hope, stopping at nearly every town along the way to post a 'missing' ad in the local papers, in which I included my cell phone number. Initially I offered a reward to anyone who might help me find my brother, but this wound up slowing me down too much, as it led to many false leads, so finally I had to ditch the reward and rely on philanthropy - and the hope that he himself would one day stumble across my ad and respond. I spent extra time in such places as Daytona, Ft. Lauderdale, Miami, and South Beach, for he had often told me how we ought to see the ocean, as no one had ever taken us there.

"South Beach was an upper-class variant of the hippie commune, I took notice, judging by the scarcity of clothing.

"Eventually I made it all the way down here, which was about as far south as I could go, with my hopes subsiding and not one single sign of him. Call it woman's intuition, or some precognitive nonsense, but something told me to just stay put; and it didn't take me long to fall in love with the place, I must admit. I used some of my inheritance to rent this cozy little pad, and to buy a sailboat to keep myself occupied, on the days I wasn't bartending at a local tavern; trusting all the while that somehow, someday, Stewart would come walking into that bar to find me."

At the mention of his name my head and Rami's shot up simultaneously, and we exchanged a startled look.

"What did you say your brother's name is?"

"Stewart," she replied. "But mostly he just goes by Stew."

"Like the soup?"

"Yes," she responded with a smile. "...Wait, you mean you've met him?"

I nodded my head. "Yes, and I can tell you exactly where you'll find him."

I broke the bad news to her along with the good, but it seemed her tale might have a happy ending after all, once all was said and done.

"Good God, and to think we were just hospitalized on the very same floor… but I need to go and see him this very instant!"

It took no time at all to hail a cab (for our cabbie was always pretty much on stand-by for us, as we were his favorite and probably best-tipping customers), and away we went.

She was tremulous as we approached his room, and we paused just before reaching it. I took her hands in mine, reassuring her, while once again advising her of his somewhat battered appearance.

She nodded and took a deep breath.

"You guys are coming in with me, right?"

"It's probably best if we don't," I said. "We didn't exactly part on the best of terms." (All the more awkward to face him, I thought, having so recently been cuddling with his naked sister, whose sweet perfume still lingered on my person.)

I kissed her on the forehead and let go her hands, gesturing encouragingly for her to go on. "Take all the time you need; we'll wait for you in the cafeteria," I told her, deciding to give the place another shot. (It had been nearly an hour, after all, since we'd had our Chinese food.)

We heard them shouting out each other's names as she walked in, and Rami and I couldn't help peeking through the narrow window outside the room.

Stew was openly weeping as he hugged his sister, who was probably matching him tear for tear, and we allowed them their privacy; low-fiving one another as we headed for some coffee - and whatever soup du jour might be featured this day.

:: Posting #38 ::

Disclosure

Summer's attention, after that, was drawn almost exclusively towards her brother, understandably. And though I still checked in on her regularly, I did so with gradually decreasing frequency.

Meantime my own compulsion toward the beautiful sea around the Florida Keys began to dwindle, and I found myself spending more time in our parked RV than I did upon our yacht, searching my soul and pondering our next course of action – for it seemed the ocean had yielded up to me what priceless treasure it had meant to.

Rami noted my introspection, of course, and generally left me to my solitude. But on one occasion he caught me studying my photo album – the original one that had been tucked away in my travel bag amidst the piles of cash – and it seemed that one of the pictures (on which my own attention had been fixed) had captured his eye as well.

"That's a nice photo, Boss," he said, tapping it with his finger. "Did you take it yourself?"

"I'm not really sure."

He gave me one of those confounded looks to which I'd become too well accustomed, reminding me of how little he still knew about me and how seldom he sought to pry. I decided to open up to him then; to make him privy, at last, to all my deep dark secrets.

I told him, in brief yet candid terms, the details of my murky background (such as I knew them); how I'd awakened in a hotel room with a severe head injury and not the vaguest recollection of how I'd gotten there. I told him about the immense cash, and the gemstones, and most important of all the precious photo album I now held. I told him, in short, the precipitating factors of our present quest, including the illusive pictures and recurrent dreams by which it was being driven.

He sat quietly for a while, allowing it to sink in – pensively, as it seemed, and not without a healthy dose of skepticism, I couldn't help but imagine. I waited patiently, nervously, for his response.

"So, our entire course is being plotted by these mysterious photographs and some vague dreams you've been having?"

I nodded my head.

"It does sound rather foolish when you say it, I'll admit. I suppose I've just been wasting both of our time. Perhaps we should just pack it all in and go home," I said, like a sulking child.

He appeared to consider this for a moment; his eyes drifting about, as usual – returning, at regular intervals, to the album which lay open upon my lap – until he reached a conclusion.

"No, Boss. I think you should keep chasing those images and following your dreams. And you can count on me to be right there with you, for as long as you need me to be."

I could have hugged him then - in retrospect I wish I would have - but it felt a bit awkward. Encouraged and emboldened, however, by his endorsement, I elaborated some more about my thoughts on the album, and the cryptic clues it might contain.

"This picture in particular has piqued my interest," I said, pointing to that of a pagoda softly aglow atop some wooded hillside; the same photo upon which he'd commented. "It's as if it's calling out to me, trying to stir some vague recollection. I almost feel if I stare at it long enough it'll start to blink. If in fact it does hold some special clue to my past, then it seems you and I will be traveling to Japan at some point."

"An Oriental excursion sounds nice, Boss; but I happen to know exactly where this picture was taken, and it wasn't in Japan. Would you like me to drive us there?"

And thus the next stop in our uncertain itinerary had been decided on, this time with the aid of my faithful driver…who was quickly becoming my dearest friend.

On the downside, the stage had been set for another difficult good-bye.

:: Posting #39 ::

Another Farewell

I picked up some Chinese food (for four) and dropped in on Summer (alone), catching her just as she was preparing to go and visit her brother, who was now in rehab.

"I'll not keep you long," I assured her. "I just need to talk to you about something."

"That's okay, my brother can wait – it's not like he's going anywhere anytime soon. Besides, I hadn't realized how hungry I was until I smelled you walking through my door."

"Well then, I hope you'll fatten me up a little before you eat me."

We spread our feast upon her coffee table, as we'd done many times before.

"So, what is it you needed to tell me? If you've come to ask me to marry you, there better be a mighty big diamond inside one of those fortune cookies."

"No, you can breathe a sigh of relief: I'm letting you off the hook. Actually, I stopped in to say good-bye."

Her hand paused for moment while filling her paper plate.

"Ah, so you're just like all those other men who save my life. First you drag me out of the ocean, then you leave me high and dry upon the beach, completely stranded and alone."

Formerly there might have been some seriousness in her tone as she spoke of her rescue, but she had gotten to the place where she could look back on it all with some levity – especially since it had led, in a sadistically serendipitous sort of way, to her reuniting with her brother.

On the several occasions we'd gotten together since that intimate encounter on her sofa, she'd never offered herself to me again. Perhaps it satisfied her unwarranted sense of debt that she had *tried* - while also making it perfectly clear, without ever saying so, that I could still claim her any time I wished. Not to say I hadn't been tempted, for the chemistry between us was real and ever present; but that was not the direction our relationship seemed destined to take. I believe we both knew that an actual affair would have ruined our friendship, in the end – just as we both knew I'd one day be moving on, whereas she had no thoughts of ever leaving Key West.

My time to move on had arrived much sooner than I had expected, in fact, and the parting was proving far more difficult than I had anticipated. Embracing that role of friendship, I shifted my focus from the emotional to the practical, asking her outright about her finances – for I meant to make good on my offer to help cover some of Stewart's mounting medical costs, if necessary.

Thankfully she did not take offense to my inquiry, though she was happy to turn me down. The inheritance from her foster parents proved far more extraordinary than I'd initially realized, even by my own exorbitant standards. It was more than enough to cover Stewart's past and future medical costs, with plenty left over for each of them to buy their own place, if they wished to – and perhaps a fancy yacht or RV for Stew, and another sailboat for Summer (for I never doubted for a moment that she'd be sailing again).

Our conversation turned casual after that, as we reminisced about our roller-coaster ride together. It concluded around the same time she polished off her food; and when all was said and done, our relationship ended as it had begun.

I stood and bowed to her, assuming an air of formality.

"Perhaps I'll see you around, fair Lady, on some distant sea or golden shore."

She bequeathed me a precious smile - perhaps refusing to be sad - and offered me her hand, which I kissed.

She still tasted of salted caramel.

"What about Rami?" she asked from her doorway as I was walking away. (Toward my personal cabbie, who had been patiently waiting for me at curbside - his meter still running, of course, though his taxi was not.)

I paused on the walkway and turned around.

"He'll be stopping by with some dinner," I assured her. "Don't be surprised if it's some more Chinese food; we didn't coordinate our menus."

"Good; I wouldn't want him to leave without hugging me. You may be the one who rescued me, but I haven't forgotten that he's the one who revived me."

I smiled and waved at her one last time.

"Yes, he's always been the true hero, without a doubt. I would have perished countless times myself without his constant protection."

She stood leaning on the doorframe for a moment - unforgettably, statuesquely.

I couldn't be sure because of the distance between us, but it seemed she might be tearing up.

"I'll always remember you, John" she said.

Then she closed her door and the memory was sealed.

:: Posting #40 ::

A Familiar Port of Call

The nice thing about living in an RV is that, come time to move, there's very little packing to be done – though Rami did bring up a very good point, once we were ready to roll.

"What about the boat, Boss?"

This stumped me for a moment. Certainly, it wouldn't do her well to sit moldering away in the marina…

The solution was as obvious as it was sudden.

"Hmm…I think I have an idea about that."

For some reason Rami always got this worried look on his face whenever I said that.

Thanks to my Captain's expert navigational skills, which transcended both land and sea, we were able to locate the dock behind Marie's house in Key Largo.

It hadn't been designed for a boat quite so large as ours, however, so Rami was barely able to nudge her up against its outer edge, onto which we dismounted via our portable boarding ladder – though not without an incident in which Rami slipped and nearly fell, hollering frantically for my help; and I had to steady him as he bridged the narrow gap between boat and peer.

"Heavens, Rami, I don't even think the water's deep enough to drown in right here; no need to panic."

"If it's deep enough to float our boat, then it's still too deep for me, Boss."

Belatedly, I realized I should have paid for some swimming lessons along the way; it was probably uncustomary to rely upon a sea captain who couldn't even swim.

Meantime Marie, who must have heard the commotion, came strolling out back to greet us – perhaps wondering if the coast guard were raiding her home. Her look of perplexity was replaced by a sunny smile as soon as she recognized us.

"Well, hello there, strangers. John, the Florida climate has treated you well: you've become quite the dashing, bearded mariner. I don't think I would have recognized you had it not been for Rami, who's as handsome as ever. I see you two have traded in your RV for a different sort of luxury liner. She's a real beauty, I have to say."

"Thanks – I don't think I've ever heard anyone string together so many compliments quite like that. And you look more dashing than ever yourself, ma'am. As for the boat, it wasn't exactly a trade; Rami still needs to go and retrieve our land cruiser. Meanwhile, permission to dock, my Lady."

"Permission granted, sailors. My neighbors are probably already seething with jealousy."

Her neighbor's boats did look rather puny, by comparison, and I cringed to think what Melanie would say once she saw it.

Her daughter wasn't home just then, Marie explained, while shepherding us inside for some coffee.

As we enjoyed what wound up being our second breakfast, Marie disclosed to us that Melanie had begun seeing someone – discreetly checking my reaction as she said so. She must have noted something in my expression, for she went on to say, with great tenderness:

"I happen to know she had very strong feelings for you, John, and perhaps you felt the same for her as well; but she hadn't heard from you in almost a year, and I began worrying about her loneliness and her sulking. I set her up on a blind date with a young real estate agent – my best friend's son – thinking she might benefit from some companionship and distraction. It worked out much better than I'd hoped, for they hit it off far more quickly and seriously than I had anticipated."

"I'm happy to hear it – I truly am," I assured her. (I couldn't believe that much time had gone by.) "We were more like best friends ourselves, really – almost like siblings."

I could see the skepticism beneath her silent nod, but she let it go.

At this point Rami, having annihilated the remainder of the homemade coffee cake, announced he'd best go fetch the RV.

"I hope you plan on hailing a cab," I told him. "I'd strongly discourage you from hitchhiking around these parts."

He caught my drift and nearly smiled.

"No worries, Boss. May I use your phone, ma'am?"

Marie and I sat out on her front porch after the cab had picked him up, conversing in a relaxed manner. I told her more or less what we'd been up to over the intervening months – omitting all the embarrassing parts, of course – until Melanie pulled up in her mother's car.

She was toting a large bag of groceries as she came strolling up the walkway and didn't even notice us at first, as we'd been sitting off to the side on a porch swing. She stopped abruptly at the top of the steps once she saw us.   I caught her eye and smiled, and her look of bemusement was quickly displaced by one of shocked recognition. She dropped her bag onto the floor – to the unhappy fate of some farm-fresh eggs - and came running over to greet me, hugging my head as she kissed it.

"Look what the cat dragged onto your porch," I said somewhat sheepishly. "Luckily your mom took pity on me and allowed me to rest here for a bit."

"Fancy that," she responded cheerily, "and we don't even have a cat. Where's your partner in crime?" she added, somewhat literally.

Before I could begin to explain, Marie got up from the swing and excused herself.

"I'll leave you two to catch up on one other. I need to clean up a little and get started on some lunch – I'm sure Rami will be starved again by the time he gets back," she said, picking up her daughter's leaking bag and heading inside.

Melanie stepped back and looked at me appraisingly, then expressed her approval.

"Hmm … you've grown nicely tan, your hair has grown out, and you've sprouted a beard. You look ruggedly dashing – I would never have recognized you, except that your bedroom eyes are unmistakable."

"Your mother used that same term – dashing, I mean - though in truth I know I look dreadful."

"No, I'd say you look delicious. But what brings you back around this way? I was beginning to think I'd never see you again. And how did you get here – what happened to your ridiculous RV?"

I decided to show rather than tell.

"Come out back with me; I have a surprise for you."

She gave me a sidelong glance but followed my lead, then let out a small gasp when she spotted the boat.

"Tell me you didn't go and buy yourself that ocean liner," she said. "I'll bet someone soaked you for an ungodly fortune."

"I guess I sort of did," I admitted. "But your mother is saving me a ton of money by allowing me to dock it here. It needs to be taken out regularly, though, or it'll grow sad and neglected and begin to rust. So you're going to have to learn to become a mariner…though I wouldn't necessarily advise you to grow a beard."

"If that's the case, I think we're going to need a bigger dock," she said, placing both her hands atop her head. "Is that really the most economical one you could find? Why does everything have to be so big with you, John?" she teased.

"It's above average, I'll concede; but you should have seen the ones I passed up," I defended.

She let drop one of her hands.

"So, will you look after her for me while I'm away?" I pursued.

"Where are you going – and why not just sell it?"

"North. And I don't think I'd get back quite what I paid for it yet, so I'd rather hang on to it and let it appreciate for a while – just like you taught me."

"I don't think it works that way with boats, John."

"Well then, let's just say I'm still fond of it, and I'd prefer to leave it with something else I'm quite fond of, so that both will still be here should I decide to return again someday."

Melanie smiled. "You do have a way of charming someone, sailor – even though you just called me a 'thing'."

She seemed to realize she'd lost the argument and won herself a temporary yacht; but then a different sort of raincloud seemed to cross her mind.

"Speaking of surprises," she said, still staring at the boat, "I have one for you as well."

(A pregnant pause.)

"I'm expecting," she said softly.

My eyes had grown wide when she looked my way, and she must have misinterpreted my reaction.

"It's not *yours*, silly; I'd be a whale by now. Not to mention almost three months overdue."

I wiped my scarred forehead in mock relief, then disclosed that her mother had tipped me off regarding her boyfriend – though not about her pregnancy.

"She doesn't know about it yet. Or probably she does, and just hasn't said anything."

She went on to tell me some more about her boyfriend – fiancée, as it turned out. (So at least he wasn't one to hit and run.)

"He's an incredibly nice guy – wouldn't hurt a fly."

I wasn't sure if the rhyme was intentional.

"I practically had to assault him just to get him to touch me," she elaborated. "He was so charmingly bashful – reminded me of you, in that respect."

(*Well, he certainly found the right spot once he did touch you*, I thought cynically.)

She leaned in close.

"You're still the best lover I've ever had," she whispered to me coyly, "so your standing with me remains intact."

I'm sure I blushed as my tongue tripped over my eyeteeth and I couldn't see what to say. *I wonder if she knows that if it* had *been mine, I would have stayed with her forever,* I thought, as I looked into her sea-green eyes.

Any further conversation was mercifully interrupted by her mother, who called out to let us know there was fresh coffee and cinnamon buns if we were hungry. We took her up on it, and we spent the remainder of our time inside with her mother, enjoying her pleasant conversation and refreshments.

At long last (though it really didn't feel so long) we heard a familiar rumble, as Rami came trundling back with the RV. Melanie greeted him with nearly the same amount of enthusiasm which she had earlier bestowed upon me, and if he didn't blush, he was certainly beaming.

The five of us (counting secret baby) went on to enjoy a leisurely dinner, during which Melanie couldn't help but boast some more about her beau (I'll be kind and spare him some fictitious epithet), unto whom she was soon to be united in holy matrimony. I learned, among his many grandeurs, that he was an expert boater – never having owned an actual vessel but renting a great many of them as often as he could afford.

"He once rented one almost identical to yours, I'm pretty certain" she boasted. "In fact, it was on one such boat that he proposed to me – on an overnight excursion to Coffin's Patch. Not the most romantically named places, I'll admit, and our expedition had to be cut short because of an approaching storm."

I exchanged a sidelong glance with Rami. *Small world,* our mutual expressions conveyed.

"He got us back safely, though," she went on to say. "He's very protective of me that way, you see, which is a quality I can deeply appreciate."

"Well then, there you have it: as official caretaker of my nautical vessel, you already have yourself an expert Captain. I'll be offended if he doesn't take you out on it on a regular basis. Might even make for a nice honeymoon adventure if you haven't already planned something. Perhaps to someplace other than Coffin's Patch, however, if you want my personal advice."

"Hmm…" she said, with a finger to her chin. "As much as I hate to prevail upon your generosity, I just might be able to persuade him of something like that. Say, if you guys are hanging around until tomorrow, you'll probably get to meet him."

From all that she had told me about him I knew I wouldn't help but like him, but I felt an urge to move on with my own journey.

"I'd love to, Mel, but Rami and I have many more miles to travel before we sleep.”

Another surprised look from Rami, but he held his silence and kept eating. Melanie, meanwhile, couldn't mask her disappointment.

Marie, as always, knew how to elevate the mood.

“Well, I'll not let anyone leave without trying some of my Key Lime pie. Not even Melanie knows my secret recipe.”

Afterward I walked out back with Melanie one last time, while Rami once again insisted on helping Marie with the clean-up. (Marie generally banned her own daughter from the kitchen, I'd noticed, but Rami was harder to say no to, and they seemed genuinely to enjoy one another's company.)

As we took a seat in the familiar gazebo, Melanie gazed out again at the conspicuous boat.

“Looks like the Titanic is still afloat,” she commented. “You know, as beautiful a yacht as she is, I think we may have to keep her docked at the marina. She's just a bit too much for our humble peer, I'm afraid.”

“I'm glad you've finally come to terms with my excellent taste, my dear. Certainly, you can park her anywhere you wish – I left the keys to the ignition with your mother. She too was leery about taking custody of her, by the way, but I convinced her it would be good for you. I found her weakness, you see, and it is you.”

She smiled appreciatively, charmingly, and I noted again how she was a youthful replica of her loving mother.

“I really am happy for you, you know, and I wish you the lifetime of happiness you so richly deserve.”

It sounded cliché, but I truly meant it.

Just above the yacht a golden sun was setting, glimmering off the glass and the chrome and the water beneath it; a replay, excluding the boat, of a previous time we had met there.

She stood up and faced me, then took both my hands in hers and lifted me gently until I was standing before her. She hugged me then, in a sisterly way: the small but palpable bump in her belly symbolizing the insurmountable barrier that had risen between her and me, separating me forever from whatever complicated romance had existed - if ever so briefly - between us; from whatever it was I had walked away from.

There was a fleeting look of sorrow in her eyes, as if she'd read my thoughts and had shared momentarily in my mixed-up feelings, but then she smiled again – catching a glimpse, perhaps, of our promising (though separate) futures.

It seemed like a happy ending; but I was already growing weary, truly, of having to say good-bye.

:: Posting #41 ::

An Unscheduled Pitstop

As we journeyed back northward, I slipped into a state of melancholy torpor, dwelling upon all those bittersweet memories we were leaving behind. But at least I was beginning to build some recollections, I told myself, which was more than I had before. My past was no longer an empty slate, in other words, and for that, at least, I felt grateful.

Of the early part of our retracement there is little to relate, as we rolled across scenery that at last looked familiar - *like traveling backward through a rearview mirror*, I remember thinking. When we reached Virginia, however, Rami surprised me with a personal request - one of the few he'd ever asked me.

"Would you mind if we took a slight detour, Boss? There's someone I'd like you to meet."

"You can navigate this beast in whatever direction you please, my good captain; you have yet to steer us astray."

We headed into the western part of Virginia (though not quite so far as West Virginia itself), which was a beautiful drive, undeniably; through rolling, verdant hills, sprawling and lush. After two or three hours we descended into a broad and shallow vale wherein a charming town lay nestled: old-fashioned, defiant, and proud - overlooked, somehow, by the normally stern vigilance of marching time.

Rami drove to the outskirts of this small town, down a winding country road that just suddenly stopped, as if it saw no need to go further.

In truth it was an idyllic setting, as we pulled up to an old farmhouse surrounded by fenced-in fields where one would have expected to see horses or cattle or *some* sort of livestock, though none were readily apparent.

Here the effects of time were more evident, as the weathered house had fallen into a state of disrepair, with an adjacent barn that had definitely outlived its finer days. Yet the entire place retained a charm that is difficult to describe - filled with stories to tell and many secrets to keep, one couldn't help but imagine.

Rami parked the RV where the road had ended, and we hopped out. He led us, whistling, through a droopy gate that creaked almost blissfully upon its hinges, then down a stone walkway which led to the houses' small wooden porch. I feared the boards might collapse beneath his weight as he climbed the few steps and approached the front door, upon which he proceeded to rap rather loudly.

"Hey, Mom, wake up! Are you home?"

Straightaway his knock was answered by a kindly-looking woman who appeared, by her facial features, much younger than I would have expected for someone of her designation, though her frame was inordinately bent from whatever untimely burdens had been laden upon it.

"Lord have mercy!" she bellowed out as she dropped her knitting needles and flung herself into her son's strong arms – who had knelt to receive her, as he was nearly thrice her size.

"Heavens, I'd been wondering what may have happened to you; crying and praying myself to sleep nearly every night," she said, punctuating every couple of words with an inconsequential punch to his abdomen.

"I mailed you a bunch of post cards, Mom. I tried calling you, too, but your phone must be disconnected."

"Sure, the post-cards were awfully pretty, but they didn't really tell me a whole lot. You could've – "

She noticed me then, for I'd remained at the bottom of the steps.

"- And who's this handsome man you've done brought me? Is this the golden-hearted young boss you've been telling me about?"

"Yes, Mom, this is John" – this being the first time I'd heard him address me by my pseudonym. "He's the one who hired me as his driver, and we've been traveling all over the place, just like I wrote you."

"Well, bless my soul," she said, appraising me with her sparkling eyes. "You must be a saintly young man to be putting up with my son, this ornery and incorrigible young rebel. I hope you've been teaching him some manners – Lord knows I tried and failed."

"We've managed to put up with one another rather well, ma'am; perhaps you've underestimated your handiwork."

She unleashed a soulful laugh.

"Heaven help me, what a charmer! But come inside, my children, before you catch your death of cold."

(It must have been 80 degrees that day, despite a pleasant breeze.)

She led us into a neat but sparsely decorated home – as though what furniture it may have once possessed had been discarded or sold. There was a significant residue of history about the place, regardless; memorialized and dormant throughout the vacant corners, like vague phantoms one could almost perceive. Lesser-worn patches along a floor or rug, for instance, where a table or a chair had once sat.

"Find yourselves a seat," she said, quite literally.

We wound up sharing a tattered loveseat that sagged significantly on Rami's end and felt a bit awkward, especially since I kept leaning into him unintentionally, while his mother shuffled into the kitchen to fetch some refreshments.

She came back shortly with a decanter of lemonade and a plateful of cornbread, setting them atop a sewing bin which she'd scooched over to us with her foot; then dragged an old rocker next to our loveseat and settled herself in, as if waiting to be apprised of all the things her son had omitted in his postcards.

She listened intently as Rami gave her a carefully edited account of our adventures, gasping and sighing and gurgling in all the right places. She seemed especially fascinated by his account of Summer's rescue and her subsequent reuniting with her brother, which appeared to have touched some special chord, and was utterly flabbergasted to learn of Rami's seafaring skills.

"Why, John, I don't know how you got him into a boat; I could never even get him to set foot in a kiddie pool: he'd go running off, hollering like a schoolgirl who'd been shown a snake."

I had difficulty conjuring such an image.

"You'd be surprised at how adaptable he's become, ma'am. I couldn't get along without him, if I'm to be completely honest."

She beamed with pride, while Rami, against who's side I'd become tightly thrust by gravity, lowered his head in modesty or embarrassment ... though I hoped he noted my sincerity.

The cornbread wound up being a mere precursor to the delectable treats that were yet to come, for she cooked us up a marvelous meal which I am unqualified to describe. I can only say it involved rice and beans and a variety of mysterious yet well-blended ingredients, which sated one's hunger long before one wished to quit savoring its delights. This we consumed once again upon our loveseat (and she upon her rocker), for nothing remained of her table but its ghost in what once had been the dining room; yet this did not diminish our enjoyment of the feast.

Afterward, being too full to move, Rami and I settled in for the night on the living room floor, on a faded area rug before the fireplace; embalmed in our sleeping bags like a couple of kids - though Rami's bag rose scarcely higher than his navel. Despite this deficit of beds, the place felt more homey than anywhere else I'd remembered sleeping, including my own home.

What the place lacked in furnishing was well-compensated for by food and hospitality, for we awoke to the aroma of a fresh-cooked country breakfast, replete with omelets and grits and biscuits with gravy, and I began to understand where Rami had acquired his culinary skills.

I was reluctant to leave this humble abode with its charming matron, but Rami insisted we not delay our journey any longer, despite my earnest protests. "Who's in charge of whom?" I pointed out.

"You're in charge of the both of us, Boss; but I'll be too fat to fit into the driver's seat if we stay here any longer."

His mother and I both nodded and smiled, and the loveseat heaved a sigh of relief as Rami stood up and reached into his back pocket.

"Before we leave, mother, I brought you a small gift."

He held out a sealed envelope, about the size of a greeting card - then pulled it back again as she reached out to take it.

"Wait ... first you must swear to me that you'll accept it."

"Well, it appears I'll have to, if I want to know what's in it."

"Okay, then," he said, and deposited it ceremoniously into her hands. "Don't open it until after we've left - and just remember, you've sworn me an oath to keep it. I'll be deeply offended and heartbroken if you don't, and everything I've ever done – and I do mean everything – will have been for nothing."

"Lord, what did you go and get me? But if it means so much to you, my dear child, then I promise you I'll use it. I hope it's a gift card to IHOP – I can't even remember the last time I've been there."

"It's not a gift card, mom. Besides, your cooking is way better than theirs."

She laughed at this, then turned suddenly sober.

"Well, you can flatter me all you want, but I'll still tell you just one more thing before you go," she said, in a motherly tone that I pleasantly sensed was intended for me as well. "I don't know what sort of mischief you two have been up to in that fancy vehicle – I know, as your mother, that you haven't told me everything – but be careful where you tread. You know full well, Ramirez Moses Alexander, where you wound up the last time you went parading around in one of those things, causing every last one of my hairs to turn prematurely grey – at least the ones that didn't drop out in sorrow. Lord help me, my child, I'd not survive another heartbreak such as that one."

She hugged and kissed him then, as he knelt silently before her, and I stood right behind him waiting my turn. And then we left, hearts and bellies replenished as we trundled down the garden path and out through the front gate - which creaked mournfully, this time, when Rami closed it.

She must have opened her card almost as soon as we'd walked out the door, for we heard her shouting and moaning and *Oh Lording* even before we'd reentered the RV.

"Good heavens, Rami, what hideous thing did you give that poor lady? It wasn't a snake, was it? You've upset her something fierce."

"Basically," he said, with a beaming smile, "I just paid off her mortgage."

We climbed into our vehicle and shut the doors, sealing out the sounds of her emotional outcry – though nevermore its happy memory.

:: Posting #42 ::

The Past Revealed (Just Not My Own)

As we drove away from that quaint little farmhouse with its endearing little occupant, Rami looked back towards me and said "You can't even imagine how good that felt back there, Boss – being able to help her out like that. All thanks to your incredible generosity towards me, of course."

I knew he'd opened a bank account (same branch as mine) into which he'd been depositing his weekly pay, and I'd never seen him buy even a single item of luxury for himself - excepting, arguably, for a nice pair of sneakers, which he'd picked up on clearance. But I hadn't realized, until then, to what purpose he'd been so stringently saving.

As he seemed in one of his rare moods to talk, I made my way to the front passenger seat, where I seldom ever sat; having to displace a good number of variably unfolded roadmaps to clear myself a spot.

"Don't sit on my maps, Boss – unless you plan on guiding us by hindsight" he said, with his quick witticism.

I couldn't see his eyes behind his shades, but a contended grin still lingered upon his lips. I couldn't recall ever seeing him so cheerful.

Over the course of the next 100 miles or so, I learned more about his background than I'd been able to glean in the entirety of our preceding travels – the summation of which is as follows. (And he gave me full consent to share it: *"I've already served my time, Boss; I can't be re-incriminated. Besides, I'm no longer ashamed of what I did,"* he assured me.)

The modest farmhouse with its adjoining barn and fields had been passed down to Rami's mother by her parents, who had inherited it from their own parents in turn – and so it had gone, through several generations past. The original inheritor had been a slave, as a matter of fact, unto whom it had been bequeathed by a kind, penitent, and childless slave-owner.

The property, traditionally, consisted of 30 or so acres of farming land, upon which a great variety of crops had been planted over the years (originally cotton), and another 30 acres of rolling pastureland over which many a sheep and cow and thoroughbred horse had grazed – the latter comprising the mainstay of the estate's income in later times.

Gloria - Rami's mother - had been a single child, just like her son, and when her parents passed prematurely and unexpectedly within a couple months of one other (farming accident, aneurysm) she was rendered a broken-hearted inheritress, single-handedly in charge of the property's affairs at the tender age of 16.

It was during this distraught and fragile period of her life that Rami's future father, Jeremy, appeared on the scene, like an armored knight on his noble steed come to save the day.

He'd been to the farm once before – to purchase a noble steed, in fact, from Gloria's parents – during which time he'd cast an admiring eye on their youthful daughter, who was about fourteen years his junior, in the same way he'd probably eyed a desirable racehorse. He had now returned to purchase a second one: only to discover, to his peaking interest, that Gloria had fallen in as sole proprietress and mistress-in-charge. Rather than leaving with another prized stallion, he wound up winning the entire stable, as it were, applying his debonair and worldly mannerism to woo young Gloria and steal her heart. They were wed within a matter of weeks of his uninvited but fortuitously timed visit.

Seizing further upon the opportunity that fortune had cast him, he had himself added to the deed and overtook full management of the estate - with Gloria's full blessings and to her own blessed relief. To his credit, he did so in a remarkably efficient and profitable manner, at first – though he chased away most of the original loyal farm hands and replaced them with others at a lesser pay, treating them with an austerity that even their ancestral slaveowners might have frowned upon.

Within a year of this opportunistic marriage two contrasting things occurred: Gloria began to understand that she'd been used, and she was blessed with what proved to be the happiest event of her lifetime - the birth of a son. (And I've obviously taken the liberty to embellish Rami's account with what I can safely assume to be the truth, as I try and reconstruct someone else's past in lieu of my own.)

Rami's arrival provided a warmth and love that had been woefully lacking in her marriage, but even as she basked in the light of her child's unwavering trust and affection, a virulent storm was darkly brewing. Rami's father, who had always made a habit of being away on business trips, began spending even lesser time at home, attending (as he always justified) to important matters in the horse-racing industry; assuring his neglected bride – now scarcely 17 – that his efforts would secure them a future of worry-free wealth and prosperity. Gloria had gently argued, to no avail, that the treasure she desired most was to have her family home together far more often than was then occurring; yet this pattern of absenteeism merely intensified over the next several years, during which Gloria essentially raised their child on her own, while Jeremy immersed himself in a covert life of drinking, gambling, and debauchery. Most of these deeds he managed to keep secret, initially, until he began showing up drunk on his occasional visits; becoming increasingly abusive whenever Gloria tried to remonstrate or reason.

Up to this time, Rami had felt a cool indifference toward his distant father; but then, as the vicious wolf beneath the fancy dress suits became manifest, he became terrified of this brutal stranger – who beat him soundly on more than one occasion when he tried to come to his mother's defense. Throughout his early teenage years this terror morphed into utter helplessness and sorrow, before rankling at last into seething bitterness and loathing. He became thankful of his father's long absences, and prayed secretly each night, to a God who seemed occupied with far more important matters, that this evil man would simply drop off the face of the planet, whereby he and his mother might have lasting peace.

Perhaps it was a deep fear for her son's safety that kept Gloria from turning to the authorities, for who can say (besides Gloria herself) what vile threats he held over her head. Rami, meanwhile, whose physical stature increased in equal proportion to his wrath, obeyed his mother's command and kept his distance – while realizing he might eventually have to take matters into his own hands, should certain undefinable lines be crossed.

He worked harder and harder around the farm, as his pseudo-father began dismissing the farmhands one by one – or simply stopped paying them, until they departed on their own; some of them seizing upon whatever property they could carry off to offset their missing wages. In due time, Jeremy resorted to selling off farm equipment and livestock to pay off his gambling debts and sustain his lecherous lifestyle, and he would likely have sold the farm itself had not Gloria's name been on the deed as well to impede it – for she preferred the recurrent beatings to the notion of signing off the remainder of her family heritage to this hedonistic and egotistical beast.

The culminating event was when, after another extended but far-too-brief an absence, Jeremy drove up to the house in a brand-new RV – with, as Rami and his mother both noted as they peered out the front window, a young Caucasian floozy (Rami's word) gloating in the passenger's seat.

Rami's mother shooed him upstairs as Jeremy waltzed up to the house, alone. For once he wasn't blatantly inebriated, and when he spoke to Gloria, his tone was nonetheless demanding but not quite so belligerent (for Rami stood listening in secret at the top of the stairs). Essentially, he was offering to sign off on his share of the deed in exchange for 60 percent of the property's remaining value. Rami noticed an insurgent fire in his mother's eyes as she raised his requested stake to 70, under the stipulation that he sign divorce papers and relinquish full custody of their son, with the further understanding that she'd never ask him for a single penny of alimony or child support.

This price may have seemed steep to some, but to Gloria and her son it felt like a bargain, and Rami held his breath from afar as he awaited the despicable man's response. His father must have been pretty strapped for cash, and perhaps he did not wish to make a bad impression on his unsuspecting new love-interest who was awaiting him in the fancy vehicle: for instead of beating her again as would have been his norm, he agreed in full to the terms she'd laid out – for he too could recognize a great bargain when he saw one.

Gloria promptly mortgaged the entire property and hired herself a lawyer, and within a couple of months she had paid off her long-term abuser and their divorce was settled under the terms they'd agreed upon.

A sense of tremendous peace and relief ensued for both mother and child as Jeremy walked out of their lives with a hefty check in his pocket, casting a look of victorious contempt at his former wife and neglected son. While it was they who perceived themselves the true victors, their tranquility was to be short-lived, for he returned just three days later with a final parting gift.

He drove up again, late one evening, in his ill-gained RV: his young floozy – who couldn't have been a week over sixteen – once again in the passenger's seat; and this time it was quite evident that both were roaring drunk. Jeremy hopped down from the driver's side, smiling toward his strumpet (my epithet) while carrying a lighted blow torch. He wandered casually into the back yard where he set fire to a beautiful playhouse which Gloria's own father had built for her when she was a child. He whooped with laughter as he watched it burn, pretending at one point to try and douse the flames by peeing into the fire.

Rami, who'd just turned 18, learned on this occasion that there are certain wounds that far exceed what a physical beating can impose; for as they stood watching aghast from the kitchen window, it was the very first time he'd witnessed his mother cry.

The invisible line, at long last, had been crossed.

As his father went laughing and stumbling back to the RV, waving and yelling out "Good-night, sweet Gloria!" when he spotted her in the window, Rami made a hasty but intractable decision. He walked to the back door and snatched, from the adjacent peg, the keys to their last remaining vehicle – a dilapidated old pickup – and, despite his mother's frantic pleas, marched resolutely from the house, resolving to follow this monster and exact revenge in some form that he could not himself as yet imagine.

He secretly but determinedly trailed them for untold miles and countless hours, stopping at a distance whenever they stopped and refueling whenever they stepped inside for food. His furor, perhaps like the smoking remnants of Gloria's playhouse, eventually cooled somewhat but his hatred and determination did not. Jeremy – still tipsy and mirthful as he toyed with his young playmate – never became aware that his son was following, with loathing in his heart and vengeance on his brain

At this pivotal point of his tale Rami took pause in its telling, for we stood ourselves in want of some refreshments and refueling. He pulled into a truck stop which featured a gleaming, metallic diner advertising homestyle food.

While awaiting our mutually preferred dish (meat loaf and mashed potatoes) Rami finished his account - which I'll conclude, as I did with Summer's, in his own words, with perhaps a bit of paraphrasing

:: Posting #43 ::

Retribution

Rami downed one of the appetizer rolls, washing it down with some cold water, before continuing his tale.

"I followed the bastard all the way into Kentucky. I couldn't even tell you what time it was, except to say it was approaching dawn, when they pulled up the long driveway of a lakeside cottage - purchased, I had no doubt, with some of the money he'd funneled from my mother's estate. I waited until they had dragged themselves inside before creeping up the driveway with my headlights off, and my plan of revenge assembled itself in a flaming instant.

"I sneaked into the RV and located my father's blow torch, retrieved his lighter from the dashboard tray, then walked to the back of the vehicle and set their bed on fire. As I returned to the front, preparing to make my getaway, I noticed that, in his tired and semi-drunken stupor, my father had left the keys in the ignition. On impulse, I decided to add some flare to my act of fury, for I was beginning to enjoy myself as I'd rarely done before.

"I'd never been inside, let alone driven, an RV, but I'd operated plenty of farm vehicles, and this one seemed pretty intuitive. So I started her up, slammed her into reverse and went screeching down the driveway, as the time for discretion had long passed. I took her for a reckless joy ride on the outskirts of the lake, scraping its polished sides along as many trees and poles and street signs as I could manage.

"The fire in the bedroom, meanwhile, gained in intensity, and before long the rear window blew out entirely. As I picked up speed the rearward flames fanned out even further, until I must have resembled a shooting comet speeding down the highway. I was sure my father couldn't have missed the show by now, but just to be sure, I smashed on the brakes, spun the flaming vehicle around and headed back towards his cottage. And sure enough, I spotted him, running frantically down his driveway. The flames at this point were beginning to worry even me, since I was the one steering that fiery torpedo: so I veered to the right, breaking through a small wooden railing. Elated by the knowledge that my father was watching, I careened down the grassy embankment and drove her straight into the lake - not once even considering hitting the brakes.

"I managed to scramble out of the driver's side as the vehicle rocked and lurched in the deep, dark water. My father scrambled to the scene just in time to see me floundering in the lake, even as his smoking RV went sinking to the bottom beneath me, sizzling and hissing as the flames were finally doused.

"I probably would have sunk to the bottom along with it (for I'd overlooked, in my adrenaline-fed exuberance, the minor fact that I couldn't swim) had not my father rushed into the lake to retrieve me - though not, as it turned out, with any thought to save me, but with every intent to beat me.

"My revenge may have been short lived, as he appeared to have regained the advantage. But what he wasn't prepared for, as he began pummeling me, were the years of accumulated rage I was more than ready to unleash. Though he was still slightly larger than I, I wound up getting the better of him, beating him to a bloody pulp till he lay blubbering on the ground beneath me, pleading for mercy – my supply of which had grown rather measly.

"As I pinned him down in a choke hold, my right fist still cocked and ready above his head, I made him swear he'd never again place slimy hand on my mother nor grubby foot on her property, else I swore to God Almighty and on my grandparents' grave that I would surely kill him.

"He stammered his assent, signing his words, figuratively speaking, with his own blood-stained spittle.

"I let go of him then and stood up, kicking some dirt onto his bleeding face as he lay panting, then headed back to my pick-up - bidding good-night to his trembling, wide-eyed floozy as I brushed passed her at the bottom of their driveway, from where she must have had a pretty good view of the spectacular events that had unfolded."

"My so-called father had never witnessed this darker side of me before, which I'd probably inherited from his own black soul. He must have believed my promise; for though he did press charges (to include theft, arson, bodily assault, property damage, and both threatened and attempted murder, as corroborated by his underaged girlfriend who falsely claimed they were still in the bed when I set fire to it), he never again stepped foot on our farm, even while I was serving my time in prison."

Here he paused once again, as the waitress delivered our steaming plates of food.

"To this day," he concluded, "I don't regret my deed in the slightest. I only regret the pain and financial burden it caused my mother."

Years of pent-up emotion must have gotten the better of him then, as he lowered his head as if to pray over his food and began to sob. I didn't know what else to do besides place a hand on one of his massive arms as he continued weeping.

"You may have inherited your father's physique," I eventually told him, "but that's where the resemblance ends, I can assure you. You have your mother's heart, and her bravery."

Our food was cold by the time we ate it, and I was disappointed they hadn't any key lime pie, but it was still one of the most satisfying meals we'd ever shared together.

:: Posting #44 ::

Homecoming

The next stop in our wandering itinerary was a brief return to Cape May, for I wished to check in on Esmeralda and provide her with another year's salary and expenses in exchange for housesitting – though I knew I'd have to force the money on her somehow.

In hindsight I probably should have warned her that we were coming; for when we pulled into my driveway late one afternoon she came running out, screaming at me in a way that expressed surprise, resentment, elation, and anger all bundled together in one explosive emotional ball, but which eventually unraveled itself as joy – though not before she had thoroughly berated me on my 'dreadfully emaciated and scruffy appearance'.

"Why did you let yourself go to the dogs, mi niño? You look as though you've been lost at sea! I can tell you never found your woman -"

She spotted Rami, then, who had wisely delayed exiting the RV, and she greeted him with all the poise and cordiality that had been missing from my own traumatic welcoming.

She was worried that the house was a mess (which of course it wasn't, it still looked as pristine as the day I'd moved in) and upset that she hadn't had time to prepare a welcome-home meal – a matter which she readily rectified, regardless, for she somehow expanded her family meal to bountifully include the two of us.

Her husband was as friendly as ever – his persistent handshake, if anything, had grown stronger – and the children all seemed to have grown as well: not just in stature, but in beauty. I quickly found myself blissfully buried at the bottom of a dog-pile, as they tugged and pulled at my long hair and beard till I had to tickle them off me one by one; all of us laughing unrestrainedly until Esmeralda yelled at the lot of us to control ourselves.

They were bashful at first around Rami – I'd forgotten that none of them had ever met him before, as he'd come to feel like a natural extension of myself – but once I'd introduced him properly, they embraced him like a long-lost uncle, and he quickly became just another part of their loving family.

After dinner we had coffee and dessert on the second-story terrace, where I soaked in the familiar vista of the ocean while listening to its soothing sighs, conveyed over the not-too-distant dunes. It all felt serenely comforting: truly like returning home, though I knew I couldn't stay for long.

Esmeralda, knowing nothing about my plans, asked casually how soon I'd like them to vacate my house. I looked back at her in confusion for a moment, until I realized what she'd been thinking.

"Unfortunately, I haven't come back for keeps just yet, mi querida madre. Actually, I've come to impose on you some more - to see if you'd be kind enough to housesit for another year, for I've many more miles to travel, I fear. The same financial arrangements would apply, of course – unless you think you might need a raise."

She appeared simultaneously saddened and relieved – sad, perhaps, that I'd not be staying, yet relieved she'd not be needing to relocate her sizeable family on such short notice. (A family which continued to grow, as I came to learn, for both she and one of her older daughters were expecting.) She insisted, however, that they didn't need any more money at all; that I'd left them with far too much to begin with, the half of which she hadn't begun to spend. Jacob, it turned out, had hired Esmeralda's husband at his hotel as well, so that their financial situation had improved.

All of which was the sort of response I'd been anticipating, but I'd find some way to work around her.

We spent the night there, on their unified insistence – though it didn't really take a lot to persuade us. They displaced some of their children, despite my protests, and Rami and I slept in one of the garret rooms – the same one that had been my favorite during the brief time that I had lived there, for its ship-like snugness and its view of the ocean. Before the night was too long spent, however, all twelve of their lovely sprites had joined us, cramped together across the hardwood floor in their blankets and sleeping bags: a beautiful, variegated, living carpet of children.

Rami proved surprisingly good with kids, keeping them awake with scary stories at which they gasped and giggled in muffled tones for fear of waking their parents and getting themselves evicted. Rami's tales were less frightening than they were silly, of course – nowhere near as terrifying, I am sure, as the ones he had lived through – but he enhanced them with a pocket flashlight: alternately shining it upward against his face or aiming it randomly at one of the children as if singling out his next victim; and I'm truly surprised we didn't all get busted. Eventually the susurrant sighs of the restless sea took over, blown in through the window on a salty breeze, and we were lulled one by one into a peaceful sleep.

On the following day I stopped in on Abe, my trusty jeweler, who – as Esmeralda informed me - had been trying to reach me all through the year. This resulted in another bounty-check for several hundred thousand dollars (my share in the sale of a few of my gemstones) with which I further enriched my bank account, much to the delight of my broadly smiling banker. While there, I removed three more stones from my deposit box to entrust with honest Abe, who seemed to be having a grand old time selling them. He was gaining international reputation as a high-end jeweler, he informed me, and though many had pressed him regarding the source of these amazing stones – including a chic Arabian Emir who arrived surrounded by a cadre of massive bodyguards who encircled him like planets around their potent sun, as he put it – the guarding of my confidentiality had been unnegotiable, and the Sultan's impressive bribes had been proffered in vain.

"He'd love to deal with you directly, though," Abe informed me, handing me the Emir's business card which was laminated in gold and put Jacob's to shame when I placed it in my wallet. "He suspects the gems to have come from the same source, you see, and he is definitely interested in purchasing the entire collection, however small or large it might be. Judging by what he paid for the ones I sold him, he'd probably offer you a hefty premium. But there was something shady in his mannerisms; something I didn't quite trust, as if he had some hidden agenda."

"Well, no worries: I'd prefer to maintain my anonymity," I said to Abe – considering I remained anonymous even to my own self. "You did well in protecting it. I have complete faith in your salesmanship, regardless: you can sell them to whomever you please, at whatever price you deem fit."

He smiled and gifted me with a thick, gold chain, which I later re-gifted to Rami, to match his watch. The necklace was of pure gold, whereas his watch was not; but he wore it proudly from that day forward.

I had grown wary of carrying large amounts of cash after our incident in the Florida Keys, but I did withdraw $25,000 in bills while at the bank. These I stashed in the kitchen freezer while Esmeralda wasn't looking, not long before we were to set sail again on our tireless journey, along with a note that read "A little cold cash for a rainy day, mi madre; use as you see fit."

One final piece of business I attended to, before leaving, was to purchase the two empty lots between my home and the sea, where some unbecoming 'For Sale' signs had recently been posted. The price was a bit steep, but well worth the preservation of the scenery.

I also stopped in on Jacob, of course, at my "birth hotel", and he too seemed elated to see me – though he failed to recognize me at first, as I'd undergone quite a 'sea-change', as he put it. He gave me a vigorous hug, along with a couple more business cards – updated, but still not nearly as fancy as the Arabian Emir's. I noted he was still sporting the diamond-studded nametag I'd gotten him, which sparkled distinguishingly against his black lapel.

The one place I purposely avoided was the tavern, where the ghost-like memories of Donna would forever linger in our former booth; for I was not yet prepared to face the deep loneliness and longing which I knew would be inevitable.

:: Posting #45 ::

The Temple Mount

Reinvigorated by my brief stop 'home', I set out once again, with Rami, on my meandrous quest: this time in the opposite direction from our maiden voyage.

Rami, the capable captain of our monstrous metallic beast, seemed pleased as punch to be employing a new set of maps – or at least the unexplored sections of some he'd already possessed – which he spread out, as usual, all about the driver's cabin. From one of the countless pamphlets and brochures he'd even cut out a picture of the Reading pagoda (the lode star of our current pursuit), which he hung from the rearview mirror as if it were a motivational beacon or a talisman.

Pennsylvania proved lovely enough (though unfamiliar) and the object of our quest much closer than I'd been anticipating; for in a matter of hours we came rolling upon the rather non-descript town of Reading, which appeared tucked and cramped within its surrounding foothills. And sure enough, near the crest of one of those hills, we spotted the bright red oriental structure which appeared, even from the distance, a perfect match to the one in my photograph.

"There she blows, Boss!" hailed Rami. "The famed pagoda. Though she looks a bit out of place in her current setting, in my opinion. Shall I try and drive us up there?"

The city traffic, both exiting and entering the expressway over which we travelled, appeared heavily congested, and I questioned whether the access road to the lofty site had been designed to accommodate an oversized vehicle such as our own.

"Perhaps we ought to conduct a reconnaissance of the area first," I suggested to Rami.

"Good choice, Boss," agreed Rami, as someone sped around our RV and then cut immediately back in front of us, narrowly making it off the expressway at the fast-approaching exit. A sign proclaimed it to be "Baseball Town", but the residents seemed better suited for NASCAR; I'd never seen so many rushed and impatient drivers.

We maintained a northerly course for a while, toward the outskirts of the harried town, and somehow wound up in a little township called "Temple" – which sounded just the sort of place one might go for inspiration and enlightenment.

Little did we know the extent to which we'd find it.

Rami pulled into a shopping complex with ample enough space to accommodate our glistening goliath, then looped around to its upper lot, which faced the same access road through which we'd entered. There we sat in the idling RV for a while, surveying our surroundings. Walmart, beyond the adjoining parking area, was the principal attraction, but there was a score of other stores scattered throughout the broad strip, distributed across two expansive lots.

Directly in front of where we sat, along the far side of the access road, stretched a raised, grassy knoll, which separated the main entryway from an adjacent McDonalds – the first business to hail the arriving shoppers, and the last to entice them before they left. Along the crest of this narrow hillock grew a lone tree, and beneath this tree sat a lone man, with his scant possessions, bearing all the hallmarks of homelessness. I had noticed him there when we'd driven in, but now, from behind the stationary privacy of our tinted windshield, I had time to study him more closely. I glanced over at Rami and saw that he was doing the same.

Our presumed vagabond was bronzed, bearded, and bedraggled, with a wizened face that was nearly lost within the great volume of hair which enshrined it. I was immediately moved by his forlorn appearance. He sat completely motionless: vigilant, yet seemingly indifferent to his surroundings, like some ancient statue or a hawk upon a wire. Whether he'd been rejected by society or had disassociated himself from it to any formal degree, he was obviously an outcast: the shade-bearing tree being perhaps his last friend and ally, at least for the moment; guarding him from the searing rays of a seething afternoon.

Even as we watched, another, similarly elderly and bearded (but slightly better-dressed) man, accompanied by one who looked to be his son, came strolling over to him from McDonalds. They had brought him a drink, as it turned out, and it was good to observe this act of benevolence amid a society that seems sometimes so overtly calloused. The father and son (as I presumed) talked to him for a while as we secretly observed, and he seemed greatly to enjoy their company – evidently much more so than the drink they had brought him, which remained untouched beneath his tree. He smiled and waved at them as they left, appearing significantly revived and animated by their temporary presence. Certainly, they had brought a brief measure of joy into his solitary day.

"Now *there's* an old man who might know something about this area," I said to Rami. "What do you think – are you getting any bad vibes?" (After the incident with Stew, I'd learned to pay closer attention to his instincts.)

Rami shook his head no and we decided to go and talk with him.

:: Posting #46 ::

King of the Mountain

The old man watched as we exited the RV, appearing surprised when we crossed the street in his direction; but he greeted us with a friendly smile as we drew near and then promptly offered us the milkshake his recent visitors had left him.

"I'm not supposed to drink those things," he insisted. "I'm lactose intolerant." He also tempted us with some pretzels from an open bag, which I likewise declined – though Rami accepted them both, by which I shouldn't have been surprised.

He introduced himself as 'Leo' – his true name, which I know he won't mind my sharing – and indeed, there was something lionesque about his appearance. What with his flowing mane of silvered hair which encompassed his head and then blended, somewhat confusedly, with his long and tameless beard, rendering his head at least twice as large as it might otherwise have been: an immense weight to be borne, it would seem, upon such tawny, scrawny legs. But there was a definite strength and compactness about him, as of one who's been used to traveling long distances. Though modest in stature, he appeared lithe, and limber, and there was not an ounce of fat to be spared upon his frame, that much was certain.

The brown corduroy shorts and plain yellow t-shirt with which he was attired had likely spent the better part of their threads on a more fortunate host, but he was in no way unclean or malodorous. Two clear blue eyes gleamed out like stars from within a creased and swarthy face, sparkling in unison with his ready smile: defying the weight of time and circumstance that had worn his body but not his soul. His possessions were few, as was evident, but he gave the impression (much like the lonely sea) of holding secret knowledge to some great and mysterious treasure which he alone could share, if only one might ask the proper question. (And forgive me for going on about him like this, but he made a deep and lasting impression on me, as you can see. Here was the first person I'd met, since the start of this narrative, whom I felt I'd known from some previous life, or stolen memory, and it's a difficult thing to describe – as was Leo himself.)

I searched for an entry-point to our conversation.

As it seemed discourteous and pointless to ask him where he lived, I asked instead "Where are you from?"

"I got here from over yonder," he said, pointing vaguely in a direction beyond his tree. "Lately I'm from right around here, though; these lame old feet don't like to carry me as far as they once did. One's world can be as big or as small as one chooses to make it, you see," he sagaciously concluded.

I nodded my head understandingly, even though I didn't.

"We're rather new around here ourselves," I ventured. "Do you know of any good places we could stay for the night?" – realizing, all too late, the irony in what I asked.

"Well, you see the tower in that abandoned feed store over there?" he asked, pointing to a remote lot across the way from the shopping center. "I wouldn't recommend that place, unless you enjoy scurrying little critters who sneak up on you while you're sleeping and nibble on your toes. I learned to befriend them, since we wintered there together, but some people are funny about that sort of thing. Lately I've been bedding down in front of that Salvation Army store right over there, which closed a couple of months back. There's a little recess in front of the store, where the sidewalk dips down to a sunken entrance, and it makes for a good hiding place. A lot of litter tends to gather in there as well, but I blend right in, so generally I'm left alone. If you just keep your eyes open and look around, in other words, you're bound to find a good spot, eventually."

I glanced at Rami, who seemed to be listening intently to the old man's every word while sipping on his gratuitous milkshake, as though we were being made privy to some priceless inside information – which I suppose we were, in a sincere though simple sense.

Already I had started to sweat, despite the shade of the tree and a gentle breeze, and I asked Leo if he'd care to join us inside McDonalds for a bite to eat.

"Sure, I have my own table reserved in there, as a matter of fact. And the foamy soap in their bathroom is the best around."

Other than a small fanny pack, the only other worldly possession he bothered to carry was an acoustic guitar within its hard-case, which he evidently took great pride in; and he brought it along into the cool, grease-laden air of the restaurant.

His 'reserved' table, it turned out, was the one right in front of the television; his "free cable", as he called it, which kept him apprised, free of charge, of the goings on in the more 'civilized' society from which he was a willing recluse.

I tried to buy him something to eat but he staunchly declined, claiming he'd eaten already – I assumed he meant today – and that he couldn't ingest another morsel. The most I got him to accept was some iced tea, which he nursed contentedly while Rami and I consumed our pernicious cheeseburgers.

Coincidentally, a news clip began to play concerning a drug bust at the pagoda.

"Have you ever been up to that place, Leo?" I asked – wondering if that's how he fit in somehow with my nebulous past.

"Just once," he said, "but I got robbed."

I couldn't even fathom what sort of person would steal from a homeless vagabond, but already I could sense that if the pagoda was somehow associated with my past, my background was already looking a bit shady.

"I wouldn't go up there alone, if you're pegging it as one of your tourists stops – but it looks like you have a pretty solid friend to take along with you," he said, indicating Rami. "I'd feel safe pretty much anywhere with him," he accurately surmised.

"So long as I keep feeding him," I responded, "he remains my loyal friend."

Meanwhile, though tempted, I didn't want to probe too much into Leo's background, since we'd only just met (insofar as I knew), so I kept the conversation casual. I asked about his guitar – a subject he was more than willing to discuss, as he promptly removed it from its case. It was a Dorado, he informed me, which he'd owned for longer than he could remember. A lovely, love-worn instrument, I could tell, and I know I won't do it justice in my attempt to describe it. Its body was light bronze, grading into an edging of burnt sienna; there were opalescent inlays between its frets, and a depiction of beautiful red roses decorated its pick guard – though the painting was faded from long use, and I was reminded for a pining moment of Donna's roses that had been left to die at the old tavern.

Soon Leo's fingers began dancing across the strings: a soft, melancholy tone that matched the sudden sullenness of my mood, as if he'd known what I'd been thinking. The other diners took pause as well to listen to him play, until he became aware of his small audience and, needlessly embarrassed, ceased his strumming.

Unexpectedly, he handed me the guitar and asked me to play something. I felt honored just to be holding his guitar, but I told him, sadly, that I didn't know how to play - then surprised myself by finding out that I could; though not nearly as good as he. I didn't even know the name of the tune I'd begun to strum, and before long the doomsaying TV had regained center stage.

We were loath, in the end, to part company, but the afternoon was wearing on, and we still needed to find a viable place to stay. Brazenly, I tried passing him a $100 bill (the smallest I had on me at the time), but he immediately passed it back.

"That's a whole lot more than I could use in one day, and I can't make change."

I didn't know what school he may have attended to become a full-time beggar, but he should have probably contacted them for a refund, I couldn't help thinking. He was a very mediocre mendicant, at best.

"Isn't there anything at all that I could get you?" I persisted. "A couple of night's stays in a hotel, perhaps?"

"No," he said with a grateful smile. "I made a couple new friends a little while ago, and I'm hoping they'll come by again tomorrow. I'll regard you two as my friends as well, if I could be so honored. Please stop back once more before you move on, so at least I'll know you didn't get yourselves killed at the pagoda," he encouraged.

We shook his hand and promised that we would, barring death or serious dismemberment.

By the time we'd returned to the RV and pulled around to leave, he was back beneath his tree; and our friendly, carefree homeless man smiled and waved at us with unfeigned cheer as we drove by in our ultra-luxurious travelling home.

:: Posting #47 ::

Dust in the Wind

"So, you want to try that abandoned silo for tonight, Rami?" I asked after we'd left the shopping center.

"You heard the sage, Boss. I don't like creepy-crawlies. There's got to be a Holiday Inn around here somewhere – I saw one in one of my brochures."

He found us a suitable hotel where we booked a couple of rooms, resolving to leave the RV in the parking lot and rent a small car for the remainder of our stay – making of ourselves a smaller target for all those brash and angry drivers.

On the very next day we drove our tiny rental (which felt like a bumper-car compared to our RV) to the hilltop pagoda, my eagerly anticipated landmark. The journey, up the sharply ascending road with its snake-like turns, wound up being more adventurous than the destination, for the site itself proved entirely unilluminating and anti-climactic.

The view from atop the hill was not altogether unlovely, as the shadows of late afternoon cast a softer sheen upon the stark city and its surrounding, over-populated suburbs; but I found nothing up there that reeked of familiarity or was suggestive in any way of my past – unless I had been a pimp or a drug-dealer in my forgotten days. Leo had been right: I was greatly reassured by Rami's proximity, else I may have been vandalized or propositioned – or both – during our brief patronage, and I was thankful we had not waited until after dark to pay our visit. We spent very little time there, to be sure, and were both quite happy to abandon it.

As we descended the summit in melancholy silence, Rami riding the brake the entire way while a trailing motorist honked his horn impetuously, I felt a sudden desire to talk again to Leo.

"You hungry for some hamburgers?" I asked Rami; and he knew exactly which ones I craved.

We parked our miniscule loaner (still reeking of melting brake-pads) outside McDonalds and traversed the grassy strip to Leo's tree, just as the endearing hobo was packing up his few things and preparing to pack it in for the night, in whatever neglected nook or cranny he intended to sleep. Even from a distance the look of lonesomeness on his grizzled face was sorely evident, but his countenance lit up just as soon as he saw us.

"Hey, guys, how are you doing? I almost got killed last night" he added abruptly, in an excited and happy tone.

He proceeded to tell us how, when he'd been sleeping in his hidden alcove the preceding night, in the sunken recess before the failed Salvation Army store, a sidewalk-cleaner had come by with his industrial sweeper; blowing an overwhelming amount of dirt, dust and debris into his receded nook and then never even stopping (a sweep-and-run) as Leo sat up gagging and coughing and gasping for air. He was already suffering from a delicate lung condition, he informed us, and had it not been for the heroic intervention of a fellow almsman, who had witnessed the sordid event and loaned him a couple of puffs from his rescue inhaler (Leo's own donated inhaler having been likewise out of breath), he likely wouldn't have survived to tell us his tale.

Appalled at the insensitivity of this sanitation worker, who surely must have noticed the distressed derelict mid the pile of debris he had propelled upon him, I asked if he'd informed anyone of this filthy deed – thinking in terms of the authorities.

"Yeah, I told my new friends about it earlier today" (I presumed he meant the benevolent father-and-son team). "They offered to take me to the hospital or the urgent care center, but I have very little faith in doctors or nurses. They just want to use my body for their weird science experiments. Last time they took so much blood from me that I looked like a prune, and they never returned a single drop. I told them that they could have my body just as soon as I was done with it, and I walked right out of the door – hospital gown and all. The last thing they saw was my butt," he concluded with a smile, "so I guess they got the message."

He had good reason to distrust a good many people, I considered, but in this case, I believed his paranoia was a bit misplaced (I'd seen what health providers had been able to do for poor Stew). Nonetheless I wasn't about to challenge him on that, as I sensed it would be futile. He still sounded pretty wheezy, however, so I asked if he'd care to join us again inside McDonalds – for though it was approaching dusk, the sun was still sweltering, and the air hung about us like thick warm soup.

"Sure! As a matter of fact, I've already secured our dinner," he said, holding up a large, grease-stained paper bag; and the three of us strode across the sun-scorched grassy strip toward the welcoming arches of McDonalds.

The bag of food which Leo bore spoke blatantly of its Burger King origins, and I worried lest this should cause some rift in the space-time continuum as we entered its arch-nemesis. Though we drew some bemused glances from the uniformed employees, nobody barred our way nor cast us out, so I ordered some McSoftdrinks to help balance the equation.

We sat at Leo's table in front of his free TV as he distributed the contents of his paper bag; and ere long we were eating whoppers and dipping Burger King fries in McDonalds ketchup with a twinge of guilty pleasure.

"I never had a whopper at McDonalds before," Rami noted after a couple large bites, "but surprisingly, they do taste better here."

This drew some laughter from Leo, though it ended in a brief coughing fit.

"You sure you're okay?" I asked, for although we'd been sitting in the cooler air for a while, he still seemed breathless.

"Yeah, I'm fine. I'm more worried about my Dorado, to tell you the truth," he said, patting the guitar case which stood propped against the table. "The poor thing took in a lot of dust as well." And then he smiled again, suddenly. "You should have heard me playing 'Dust in the Wind' a bit earlier, though; it was like I was creating my own special effects."

He had a way of finding the positive in almost any situation, it seemed, and already my recent somber mood had subsided. "Here's a man I ought to be helping," I thought, "and instead he's helping me."

"So, have you guys completed your daring pilgrimage to the pagoda?"

I told him about our disappointing visit; and once again, it was ironic how this homeless man, with no apparent family and so few possessions, was able to console me and brighten my mood.

"I've travelled many places that didn't live up to my expectations," he said. "I guess that's why I kept moving on. Just don't give up – I'm sure you'll find that special place if you just keep looking, and never linger any longer than you need to. There are still a few sites I'd like to see myself, matter of fact; but though my spirit is willing, my body is weakening."

I nodded my understanding as I gnawed on a fry, and then ventured to ask:

"Where are you from…originally?"

He gave us a few details, but they were sketchy and brief.

Turned out his family had emigrated from Portugal and settled in the northeastern part of the country – somewhere in Massachusetts. (He spoke a few words in Portuguese, at Rami's request, and I was astonished to find that I could understand him – which sent my mind on a tangent of its own, as I speculated on how this could be possible.) When later I sought more specifics about his family, a dark shadow seemed to pass before his eyes, and it was his turn to wax quiet and introspective.

From what little he was willing to share, something dark and tragic must have happened when he was about twelve years old which split his family apart; for it was then that he'd set out on his own, wandering from place to place along endless railroad tracks, and had completely lost touch with his relations. He'd travelled as far as the Carolinas before returning north – though never so far as his childhood home – and had settled himself, eventually, in Pennsylvania. He'd even lived in a small apartment for several years and had worked long enough, in a shoe factory (now long defunct), to earn himself a small social security stipend – which was deposited monthly to a personal account, accessible automatically by his debit card. Upon retiring, however, he could no longer afford both food and lodging, and had opted to forgo shelter and live freely in the open air, as he'd been forced to do in his younger days. He never liked being walled in anyhow, he explained – "If the animals can survive outside, then why can't I?"

"I've always known the value of a good pair of shoes," he concluded, "which is why I worked in a shoe factory."

A simple, humble, and practical man, who accepted each day as a gift and lived it out by faith.

After a respectful pause and some additional contraband fries, I gently asked: "Do you know if your parents are still alive?"

He appeared to consider this for a moment.

"My father returned to Portugal, with my siblings, so I don't know. I asked to go along with him, but he said my hair was too long, and that I was too much of a 'Mama's boy'."

A remembered pain became evident in his misty blue eyes, and then quickly passed.

"He'd be nearly 100 by now, so I suppose he's dead. As for my mom, she stayed in Massachusetts, with her new boyfriend – never knowing my father had left me behind. I knew her boyfriend cared even less for me than did my father, so I stayed away."

He grew quiet again for a little while before continuing.

"I think my mother may have recently died, though. When somebody close to you passes you can feel it, you know, no matter the distance; and last year I felt as though a piece of my spirit had been borne away."

He closed the mental book on the subject after that; staring at the TV without hearing a single word the newscaster was saying, I was sure.

:: Posting #48 ::

A Fellow Castaway

I was moved by the old man's tale, both for its intrinsic sadness and for the fact that I could relate to his loneliness, to some extent. During the ensuing silence I devised a plan – a proposal, to be exact – which I intended to lay upon him before we left the region. (Which would probably be in the very near future. I had something of the nomad in myself as well, you see, and already I was feeling the urge to move on; there being very little, other than Leo himself, to compel me to stick around the area for very much longer.)

"So, Leo," I eventually said, attempting to lighten the mood, "now that we've crossed the Pagoda off our list of prestigious local tour stops, where else would you propose we visit before leaving Reading?"

He smiled, and some of the extra wrinkles disappeared from his brow.

"The very best thing about Reading," he informed us, "is everything that isn't in it – which is why you won't catch me in one of their homeless shelters ever again. My standards may seem low, but theirs are even lower, I can tell you."

A secondary idea occurred to me then.

"Tell you what, Leo; how about you serve as our personal guide over the next few days, and show us all the best this area has to offer?"

He seemed flattered by the proposal.

"Do you really mean that?"

"Of course – I'd even offer to pay you, but I know I'd be wasting my time. I hereby designate you our free tourist guide. No professional references required. Are you available to start tomorrow?"

He nodded and we shook on it, and the deal was done.

"Shall we meet you back here in the morning – or would you like to come over to our hotel, and catch a little break from the Grim Sweeper?"

"Nah," he said, "I'll keep taking my chances in the great outdoors. Most of the hotels around here are crawling with bedbugs, anyhow."

My skin felt suddenly itchy, and Rami began scratching the back of his head.

Leo wound up being a most interesting and entertaining tour guide. Rather than taking us to what most would consider your traditional travel destinations, he showed us instead the exclusive world in which he lived and survived, on the unsheltered fringes and outskirts of civilized society.

I insisted he sit in the front passenger seat of our rental car, next to Rami, so he could more easily provide him with directions. Consequently, Rami quickly became used to making sudden stops and turns (for Leo seemed easily distracted), whereby we began to fit right in with all the other drivers who held a common and irresistible fascination for the sound of their own horns.

The first place Leo led us was to a bright red food-and-fueling station which, as he claimed – and we were able to confirm – served the best-tasting coffee around. (The taste of coffee, as I have learned, being a relative thing; varying in correlation to the company with whom it is consumed.) The well-frequented business also housed one of his fellow hermits, who practically lived at one of the gas station's outdoor tables – where one might enjoy one's coffee and refreshments while inhaling the fresh fumes from the nearby fuel pumps.

Leo's fellow almsman went by the moniker of 'Tuffy': presumably for his ability to survive for as long as he had under the circumstances in which he lived, for he appeared to be even older and more weather-beaten than Leo, who was himself pushing seventy. Tuffy was a jolly, rather chubby, if somewhat odd old chap, with long, snow-white hair and beard, and dressed, as we met him, in a raggedy red jumpsuit. He cast an unmistakable resemblance to Santa, truth be told – if you can picture a Santa who smokes like a chimney, curses like a sailor, and argues incessantly with a host of invisible strangers by whom he is invariably surrounded. This Santa was plagued with the company of demons rather than elves, it would seem, and he showed trust in no one aside from Leo – though he tolerated our presence at his table after learning we were Leo's friends. So, we sat and sipped on Reading suburb's best warm beverage while listening to the unique dialogue between two seasoned old hobos, which was frank and earnest in its simplicity. (When two homeless men chat about the weather, for instance, the implications are anything but casual, and the subject of food and dining is a matter of abiding hope and faith.) Still, their conversation was sometimes difficult to follow, being frequently interrupted by Tuffy's rude and invisible companions, towards whom he responded with the most abrasive language you could imagine. This being sometimes misdirected at a passing stranger, who became the unintended recipient of his offensive tirade. I was frankly surprised he didn't get himself clocked by one of these passersby, but evidently, they were either accustomed to him, or they quickly perceived that the old man was completely unhinged and disregarded his insults. Regardless, he was Leo's compadre and protégé, so we accepted his eccentricities and treated him with respect. They were starkly different from one another, in their personalities and comportments, yet their predicaments were essentially the same: two shipwrecked old sailors, adrift on the uncertain seas of homelessness; relying on whatever bounty the capricious winds or currents might bring their way, which they never hesitated to share with their fellow castaways. There was a code of ethics between these veteran vagabonds, in other words; a trustworthiness and reliability which far superseded the tenuous bonds that exist among many of society's wealthier and more privileged, who seem hell-bent on outdoing one another.

This I learned over a single cup of delicious coffee.

:: Posting #49 ::

Long Forgotten Tales

In addition to this gaseous and charming little eatery tenanted by Santa's alter-ego, Leo directed us, in his stint as tour guide, to several of the favorite nooks he had found throughout his local ambulatory travels; little hideaways to which he sometimes retreated when he wished to get away from the madding crowd, on whom he nevertheless depended for survival.

He had a secret fishing hole for instance on the back side of a hidden lake, inaccessible by road or common pathway, in which you could catch a fish almost as often as you could dip your hook. We wound up purchasing a tent and camping out there for a couple of nights, just the three of us, cooking the best of our catches over a campfire while enjoying the solitude of nature and the eclectic witticisms of our wise old host.

Less secluded but no less lovely was an arboreal park on the expansive grounds of a local museum, on the outskirts (and hence one of the less hazardous parts) of town, wherein a particularly lovely garden was nestled. Devised and donated by some loving brother in honor of his prematurely departed sister, it housed a magnificent variety of plants and flowers, artistically compiled and landscaped; but most impressive were a pair of giant windchimes hung high from the branches of some massive trees. It was as if, with each passing breeze, Mother Nature piped her otherworldly, plaintive tunes through these mighty instruments, soothing the casual wanderer who might have paused to rest in one of the shaded benches underneath. Something in this mournfully charming place, and in the random tunes of the giant windchimes, seemed to connect with Leo's soul, as we sat listening with him, in reverential silence, for minutes on end.

From there he led us to another of his magical locations: the back parking-lot of a rug and mattress warehouse, where sometimes unsaleable carpet remnants and even entire mattresses were tossed until they could be hauled away, creating a temporary oasis in which a homeless man could sleep — so long as he sneaked in after hours and left before daybreak, lest the unsuspected arrival of the trash truck compress all his remaining days of sleep into a single night. We passed on his invitation to stay overnight, however, despite his assurances that the discarded mattresses were previously unowned and hence completely free of bedbugs.

On another occasion he showed us the train tracks along which he had originally hiked, from that far northerly direction toward which he had never dared return. It was an ordinary track, on a gravelly mound which receded through an endless procession of trees, but to him it seemed almost sacrosanct. He peered dreamily, if somewhat warily, up its straight and unending trail, as if trying to catch some fleeting glimpse of his haunted past.

Of all his sanctuaries and hideaways, however, his self-proclaimed favorite was an abandoned quarry to which he adventurously led us — clearly marked as dangerous and off-limits by a host of *No Trespassing* signs which he seemed to interpret as *"Open 24 Hours: No Shirt, No Shelter, No Problem."* Rami and I were skeptical about entering, but Leo assured us there was no one actually patrolling or enforcing this no trespassing zone, so we followed him down a steeply descending pathway through the woods behind the railway.

We descended into a beautiful little valley, invisible from any surrounding roadways, with sheer cliffs which precipitated into a manmade lake with opaque, cobalt waters: darkly colorful, but impenetrable. The creepy, unfathomable depths of this lake, claimed Leo, concealed the bodies of countless missing persons — victims of unsolved crimes and murders that occurred in the city on a regular basis.

"This place is truly haunted," he explained. "The voices of lost souls speak to me sometimes, and I always try and listen, because I think they're looking for someone to help solve their murders so they can rest in peace. But who's going to believe a crazy old tramp like me if I share their whisperings? Tuffy does, of course (though he refuses to come down here), but the cops never do; they just look at me and laugh, suggesting that I should check myself into the loony bin, or jump into the lake and join my haunters. Still, I continue to listen, and try and console them, for I can understand their loneliness and sorrow. Nobody really wants to be forgotten once they're gone."

I never heard any voices myself while we were down there, but the place gave me the willies, and at one point I noticed that Rami was looking rather pale, in a relative sense. (Later, he confessed to me that he had heard the voice of a child, but I suggested to him it might have been an echo from someplace above.) Still, I had no doubt that Leo was being truthful and sincere in what he said, and I told him so – which brought a couple of appreciative tears to his watery blue eyes.

I could understand his connection to these forgotten victims, if indeed they were down there: like Leo himself, and perhaps countless other homeless people, they had an unfinished story to tell, which might never be heard or concluded.

I hoped Leo's tale was not yet finished, and that there'd be someone who would listen to it, and pass it on, in a much more skilled and thorough manner than I have done.

:: Posting #50 ::

Stable Housing

At this point I should note, just for the record, that my diary has finally caught up with the present, surpassing that point in time when I first began recording and posting these memoirs.

We stayed at the Holiday Inn in Reading for many more days than I otherwise would have, in part so I could bring my memories up to date and post them on social media (for which purpose I purchased a much more powerful than necessary laptop), but more so as an excuse to keep in touch with dear Leo for as long as possible, as he remained a perpetual source of inspiration and wisdom. It should make no difference to my narrative, except that the memories I'll henceforth be recording will be much more recent, and my postings – now that they are closer to real-time – will occur with less frequency.

But back to my (more recent) past.

As instructive and amusing as were these excursions with Leo, the highlight of it all came at the very end, when he informed us, while we were picking him up one morning at his favorite tree, that he'd found himself a home. A "cabin in the woods", as he described it. He was eager to show it off to us, in fact, so we ordered our breakfasts to go and drove to the location.

It really wasn't all that far – within fairly easy walking distance, for Leo – and nor was it nearly as remote as I had initially envisioned.

We pulled off the busy highway onto a dirt lot, alongside a closed and defunct garden supply store with graffitied walls and broken windows. From there he led us a brief way, on foot, into an overgrown area behind the abandoned building, where, hidden amongst the overspreading weeds and saplings, stood an old, dilapidated wooden storage shed – presumably an adjunct to the original property.

"Here's my new mansion," he boasted, as he led us through a doorless entryway.

He had already staked his claim, as his tattered old sleeping bag lay spread across the middle of the plywood floor; and his beloved guitar, secure within its case, was propped against the back wall. The wooden structure was cracked and warped in spots (much like Leo), but at least the roof appeared to be intact and there were no obvious signs of leakage (again like Leo).

"Here, let me show you around," he said; and he stood in place and did a little pirouette. "So, what do you guys think?"

Rami, who had to stoop at an awkward angle to avoid the wooden crossbeams, nodded his head in an oblique but approving manner.

"It looks rather spacious," I augmented, "especially with the simplicity and sparsity of your furnishings. You could probably fit a whole second hobo in here, quite easily."

"Thanks," he responded with a proud smile. "And I can stay here, rent-free, for as long as I want to…or at least until I get caught."

We celebrated by sitting together on the plywood floor and enjoying our breakfast which we'd brought along from McDonalds; a simple yet delicious house-warming feast, commemorating a simple yet magnificent shelter. (Though it needed very little warming, truth be told, as the morning heat had already begun to mount; and I imagined the place would be pretty stifling come early afternoon.)

It was on this occasion that Leo also announced his official retirement from his brief career as tour guide, there being nothing further in the area he deemed worthy of showing us.

I wondered, too, if he was loath to leave his new home; but if so, he was a very early riser, for it was under his usual tree, near McDonalds, that we still found him the next couple of mornings. I finally figured out that, despite his solitary lifestyle, what he loved most was being around people, and talking to whomever might lend him the time of day.

Companionship and conversation, I realized, were the only donations that he truly craved.

:: Posting #51 ::

Proposal

Despite, as I've already noted, the pleasure and enrichment we'd been receiving from Leo's friendship, my urge to resume my own personal journey was becoming irresistible – especially since Leo had finished disclosing to us the area's best coffee vendors, public bathroom soaps, and secret, seldom-frequented hideaways. And even more importantly, since he had finally found himself some 'stable housing', as he had termed it.

Still, I dreaded breaking the news to Leo – though I meant to follow it up with another proposal I had previously devised.

In the end, it was Leo himself who brought up the subject, as we sat sharing some morning coffee and powdered donuts with him beneath his tree. (Refreshments I had picked up at Santa's fueling station along the way, as we'd needed some gas for our rental car. I'd deposited a Twix bar at Santa's table on our way out, having discovered this was his favorite breakfast, and he'd taken pause from caustically lambasting his personal demons just long enough to chuckle and thank me and to send his prayers and regards to Leo.)

"Tuffy says hi, by the way," I told Leo, remembering to deliver Santa's message – minus all the expletives.

"He's a crazy old loon," he responded affectionately. "Who else would get away with chain-smoking cigarettes at a gas station?" And then he looked at me suddenly with his sparkling blue eyes and said, "I imagine you two will be moving on pretty soon."

"Was I thinking out loud?" I responded, "Because you snatched the words right out of my mind. To be perfectly honest, Leo, we're planning on journeying northward real soon – perhaps as early as tomorrow."

I paused for a moment to allow this to sink in; wiping some beads of sweat that had already begun to gather on my brow. It was quite humid as well, and the morning dew was slow to evaporate.

Leo's eyes looked distant.

"Tell you what, old buddy," I said, deciding to lay all my cards on his tree roots. "Why don't you join us for a while as we head up north? We could find out, once and for all, about your mother."

He quickly shook his head and said no, as if I'd just tried to slip him another $100 bill. But then he lowered his gaze and appeared to think about it some more, as I waited in hopeful anticipation; the sweat, once again, overspreading my brow.

Perhaps it was his recent near-death experience which prompted him to take action; to avail himself of an opportunity that might never again present itself.

He finally looked up to me and said, "Are you sure you wouldn't mind dragging along an old tramp like me?"

"You already proved yourself worthy company as our tour guide; I'd be delighted if you joined us," I assured him – making it seem as though we'd been planning on heading northward all along.

I looked over at Rami, who had stopped being surprised at my sudden decisions, and he nodded his agreement while finishing off my share of the powdered donuts.

We arranged to leave around noon the following day, which would allow us some time to return our rental, pack up the RV and check out of our hotel.

"Meet you tomorrow around lunchtime, then, beneath the golden arches?"

"I'll be there with my bag packed," he said with a wink.

:: Posting #52 ::

The River of Time

Preparations having been executed as planned, we arrived at McDonalds at the appointed time, parking our megalithic traveling home in the same spot as on that first day we'd met Leo.

He wasn't beneath his tree, nor did we find him inside the restaurant; and I began to worry that he'd changed his mind about coming along.

I bought Rami one of his Happy Meals (two Big Macs, a vanilla milkshake, and a supersized fry) and we sat at Leo's table beneath the TV, hoping he'd come along before too long. And sure enough, in as little time as it took for Rami to polish off his first hamburger, in he walked, looking rather dapper: wearing what looked like a brand-new pair of brown Bermudas, a flashy, Green Lantern T-shirt, and a black, oilskin cap that did little to contain his wild hair – merely drawing more attention, if anything, to the magnificence of his beard. He had his guitar, of course, his rolled up sleeping bag, and his knapsack, and some unknown items in a small plastic Walmart bag, but that was the extent of his personal luggage.

I greeted him with the same cordiality and alacrity he always extended toward us when he saw us, and he reciprocated in kind.

"We saved you a spot at your table, Leo – though I almost didn't recognize you in your fancy ensemble. Do you want a little bite before we leave?"

He told me, as usual, that he'd already eaten; but there was something else on his mind, I could tell.

"You okay?"

"Yeah, I'm just disappointed that I didn't get to tell my other two friends I'd be leaving for a while, in case they should come looking for me."

We knew he'd kept in touch with the father-and-son team whom he'd met on the same day he met us, for we'd seen them talking to him beneath his tree on a couple of occasions; but we'd kept our distance, not wishing to intrude, and so we'd never gotten to meet them ourselves.

"Well, I don't imagine we'll be gone all that long, and I promise to deliver you right back to your tree, long before too many of its leaves have fallen. And just think of all the new stories you'll have to tell them."

He seemed sufficiently reassured by this, and before long we were headed out to the RV, which was gleaming like a black diamond in the blazing sun. (Thankfully, Rami had used the remote starter before we'd left the restaurant, else we'd have been like Shadrach, Meshach, and Abednego, walking into a furnace.)

Leo had seen the outside of our vehicle before, but he stood in muted awe when he climbed inside, as though he'd been granted admission to an alien spacecraft. He took great care not to touch anything, and he wouldn't even sit down without asking permission.

"My shed is your shed," I assured him. "Mine just happens to be a traveling tool shed; don't be fooled by all the fluff and polish."

Still, he tucked himself into the far corner of the sofa, behind the table, from whence he seldom moved once we started, staring out the window at the passing scenery as if beholding the world for the very first time.

He spoke not a word for the longest while before snapping out of his reverie, as if suddenly recalling that he wasn't alone.

"So, what draws you guys northward? Are you seeking another picture-worthy landmark, like maybe a lighthouse? There are some beautiful ones along the northern coast that would put our pagoda to shame, I hear."

I could have gone along with that hypothesis or invented some other excuse, but there was something about the old man that compelled me to be honest. It seemed to me he was as trusting, in his simplicity, as he was trustworthy, once you secured his friendship, and I could see no harm in telling him the truth.

He listened intently as I told him the same tale I'd revealed to Rami just a couple of weeks prior; and this time Rami did not cast me any wary glances as he had when I'd gotten a little too loose lipped with Stewart. When I'd finished, this humble man seemed as deeply moved by my life's story – such as I knew it – as I had been about his, though his own circumstances seemed so much worse. He looked lost in thought for a while, his forehead creased, before offering me the following.

"We have a lot in common, you and me. It seems both of us have lost our pasts. I hope, once you find yours, it'll be worth remembering. There are things about mine I would definitely like to forget, but I imagine it would be even worse to have no memories at all…"

It was my turn, then, to sit staring out the window, as I thought about what he said. Certainly, he'd struck a note of truth, for as determined as I was to seek what I had lost, there was a part of me that feared what I might find.

Ten miles, ten minutes rolled by without either of us speaking, and I decided to break the silence.

"I'm glad you chose to come along, Leo; I really enjoy your company. I hope you're finding the accommodations to your liking so far?" I asked, a bit tongue-in-cheek.

He smiled at this.

"Well, normally I don't like being stuck inside four walls and a roof, but I like the idea of a house that travels. I'm not much different, in that respect: my body is my home, you see, so I take my house along wherever I go as well."

He appreciated ironic humor, it appeared, and could dish it out as well as he could take it.

"I suppose I was born to be a wanderer," he went on to say. "Still, these tired old feet have walked nearly far enough, and these jaded eyes have seen about all they care to see. I doubt if my brain could store much more. That's another thing you should know about memories: once your mind is full of them, you need to forget a few to make room for the new ones. I find it best, then, to try and discard the ones I'd rather do without – though that's not always easy. Of course, you don't have to worry about that just yet: you're young, and your brain still has plenty of storage room. Some of your memories have become mysteriously locked away, however, so in a sense you're rewriting your past even now. Perhaps, in time, these new memories are the ones that will matter most. Even so, I can understand your desire to recover whatever it is you've lost."

We watched the scenery for a while as it rolled steadily past our windows.

"Believe me," he continued, "there are things from my own past I wish I could get back, and people I wish I'd never walked away from. But as fondly and longingly as I may remember them – *saudades* is the unique term for this bittersweet emotion in Portuguese – they remain beyond my reach."

Another pause, as the outside world continued reeling itself in, like film upon an endless spool.

"Time is like a mighty river: it flows in only one direction, and the current is strong. Be careful whom you choose to discard or abandon along the way, for no matter how badly you may miss them later on, you might not be able to go back and retrieve them. Not only would you have to fight against the current, the one you seek may have already been carried along on a course of their own. Along a different tributary, you might say, and it's only by fate or good fortune that your paths may intersect again one day. And even then, who's to say that you both will not have changed beyond recognition?"

He fell silent again, as his eyes grew distant, and I supposed there was someone (or ones) he'd been thinking about as he offered his unique perspectives. Certainly, there were already some people in my own abbreviated past unto whom his metaphors could apply.

A young couple flew past us in a convertible, heading the other way (different paths, different tributaries), smiling and waving and giving us the thumbs up. Enjoying life and creating their own memories. This drew both of us back into the present, and Leo caught my eye and smiled.

"Don't put too much thought into the words of an old fool like me. Perhaps the most important thing you need to remember is this: the destinations we seek may wind up mattering less than the paths we choose to get there."

:: Posting #53 ::

Mashed Potatoes

Such were the pearls of wisdom strewn by Leo along the way, and I'm glad I wrote some of them down in one of my photo-journals so I'd remember them properly.

Rami, meanwhile, expert as he was in navigating life's convoluted highways, kept us steadily on course, and we crossed the state line into Massachusetts around suppertime. (Or dinnertime, if you'd prefer: it's all the same to Rami and me, so long as it involves food.) He reminded us how hungry we all must be – speaking mainly for himself, of course – and I left it up to him to choose our dining hole.

Before long he pulled into a gleaming, roadside diner with an oversized parking-lot wherein numerous trucks were auspiciously gathered. Quoting directly from the slogan upon their sign, I convinced Leo to join us in a 'good, old-fashioned homestyle dinner'. (Or supper – he had no preference either, as both were equally rare to him.)

We followed in the wake of a stout, grandmotherly-looking waitress as she guided us to our table. She spoke loudly and welcomingly, and we could tell by her grammar that she was accustomed to interacting with truckers. No sooner had we been seated than we found ourselves equipped with similarly ample-sized menus which she seemed to have produced out of thin air. Leo stared at length at its illustrated pages, appearing as overwrought as a child having to choose between 31 flavors of ice-cream, until finally he put down the menu and said, "I'll just take whatever it is you guys are having, I guess."

Only Rami ate more dinner rolls than he as we awaited our entrees; our waitress efficiently refilling the breadbasket like a magician producing objects from seemingly empty hats and scarves – or in her case, a very large apron. The food proved well worth the wait and was delivered in trough-sized platters and bowls rather than plates.

I don't know what came over me while we ate (nor why), but I found myself staring at the generous serving of mashed potatoes that was heaped upon my plate as if I'd never seen such a thing before. I was intrigued by the incidental shape it formed, for it reminded me of some object that was just beyond my conscious grasp. Something, I assumed, from within the locked and damaged portion of my brain – which was the vast majority of it, I'll be the first to admit.

I began sculpting the potatoes with my spoon: deliberately, intently, and the illusive image I was trying to retrieve was beginning to take shape – but not quite. I flagged down our obliging waitress and ordered three more helpings of potatoes which I began adding, strategically, to my first – much to Rami's deepening embarrassment and Leo's rising intrigue, for my mound of mashed had grown quite mountainous.

Some children at an adjacent table (for not all the hungry diners were truckers) could not contain their amusement and began pointing at us and snickering. One of the youngest – a cute little sprout no more than three – tugged at his equally red-headed mother's sleeve and asked her outright, "Mommy, I thought you said it's bad manners to play with your food; how come he gets to do it?" The young mother looked over, did a double-take, and I smiled at her innocently. She turned quickly away and whispered to her child that staring was impolite as well, and that he should mind his own business – though I noticed she'd been unable to keep herself from smiling back at me, in that manner that had become so customary toward me from the opposite sex.

I ignored them all and returned to my own business as well, for I was making some real progress.

"Are you going Close Encounters on us, Boss, or have you decided to take up food sculpting?"

I nodded my head irrelevantly and kept on working, for I could sense I was almost there. A little more rounding off at the teetering top, a little detail-work at the base with my fork, and – yes, I believed I had something! Only I didn't know what...

Leo came to my rescue then, for he seemed to have tuned into my vision. He scooped up his own potatoes, which he had scarcely touched, and added a smaller mound at the base of my larger one. "Voila!", he proclaimed. "It's the Pão de Açúcar!"

"The pound of what?" asked Rami.

"The Sugarloaf Mountain – a famous landmark and tourist attraction in Rio de Janeiro, Brazil. If you thought the Pagoda was something, you haven't seen anything, yet. Neither have I, for that matter, but I've always wanted to go there. They speak Portuguese down there as well, you know."

There could be no doubt it was the exact shape at which my mind had been groping. I had even recognized its Brazilian name when Leo had spoken it.

Rami must have recognized the look in my eye (else he read my mind outright), for he glanced at me and said "Okay, Boss; just don't expect me to drive us there this time."

Leo laughed at this, then held his arms out perpendicular to his body, as if miming an airplane. This to the further amusement and laughter of the nearby children – and even their parents, who could no longer constrain themselves from looking.

"Okay, I get it," I said. "We're going to have to fly."

"No – well, yes," said Leo, "unless you have a boat. But I'm impersonating Christ on the Mountain – another of Rio's famous landmarks which you'll have to visit on my behalf."

I set down my fork and stared proudly at my sculpture – would have snapped a picture of it, in fact, had I not left my camera in the RV.

"Are you going to finish those mashed potatoes, Boss?" asked Rami.

I passed him my plate and told him to have at it.

My masterpiece had been completed, after all, and its subject made plain; I could see no need to save it.

At our neighboring table, three miniature replicas of my potato sculpture had already been cast.

:: Posting #54 ::

Closure

In any event the Pão de Açucar, unlike my pile of mashed, would keep for another day. Meantime, we had more pressing matters to attend to.

We arrived just before dusk in the little town of Chicopee, Massachusetts. It was one of those rare occasions in which Rami had not preselected our campsite, and we wound up parking alongside a lovely, wooded park near the center of town, figuring we could just open all the windows and forego the usual hook-ups for the night. Fortunately, there was a public toileting facility nearby, and there was little in our fridge that would go bad any faster than we could eat it. Another advantage was that we were near the city's courthouse and public library, where we planned to begin our search for Leo's mother on the following day.

We sat in the park in the shade of a tree for a while, finishing off the chocolate milk and vanilla ice cream, while Leo strummed some soulful tunes on his Dorado. Some of the locals, who had been relaxing or strolling about the park, drifted over to listen to him play. A few even tried to drop coins into his open guitar case, but he smiled at them and waved them off.

Tough to lose that beggarly image, it would seem, even while touring in a million-dollar RV.

It was a pleasant way to end our day and sleepiness crept in not long after the sun had set, so we opted to turn in early.

Leo declined to have me convert the sofa into a bed for him, claiming he'd have great difficulty sleeping in anything that comfortable; but I showed him which buttons to push before retiring to my room just in case he should change his mind. When I came out a while later to grab a bottle of tepid water from the refrigerator before plunging into my own luxurious bed, however, I saw that he'd taken his tattered old sleeping bag and lay curled beneath the table, where he appeared to be sleeping in perfect comfort.

He probably slept better than I did, in fact, for my night was restless, thanks to a recurring dream in which I was trying to climb the Sugarloaf Mountain but kept sinking down into its mashed potato-like consistency. I tried crawling, creeping, running, and leaping, but to no avail: essentially, I was Sisyphus, minus the boulder.

Morning came and freed me at last, as I was stirred from half-sleep by Rami's panicked voice outside my bedroom door.

"Wake up, Boss. Leo's gone missing!"

I removed the pillow from atop my head and rolled out of bed, unconcerned.

"Check underneath the table," I told him.

Turned out he was no longer there, however, and neither was his sleeping bag.

Neither of us were concerned, even for an instant, that he had pulled a Stew and absconded with anything of value, for we both knew he'd be incapable of such a thing; we were just worried that he might have gone on his way without saying good-bye.

Our fears were soon relieved, however, for we found him sleeping soundly on a nearby park bench beneath an elm; at one with nature and his preferred surroundings.

Rami and I looked down on him for a moment and then looked at one another and smiled.

"Let's wake him up once breakfast is served," I suggested.

We took a short walk to a ubiquitous McDonalds and ordered some sausage sandwiches and coffee to go. Leo was awake when we returned, and he made room for us on his park bench. We enjoyed our meal right there, in the open air, mid the birds and the squirrels (with whom Leo shared) and the pleasing clemency of a Massachusetts morning.

Afterwards, we set about on our quest for Leo's past. This wound up taking far less time than had my own thus far, for we found his mother just two hours in, at the local library. (In a newspaper article, that is, of the library's digital archives.) Leo's instincts had been correct, however, for she had died just a few years prior — almost to the very day, ironically enough.

Leo kept silent as Rami drove us to her final resting place, and I imagine it felt to him as though he were being driven to a funeral. The destination proved to be quite lovely: an arbored graveyard aside a rural church, overlooking some rolling hills and farmlands.

We strolled slowly, deferentially, all about the cemetery, studying the various gravestones; some of which dated back to the 18th Century. It was Leo, unsurprisingly, who first spotted her simple stone marker.

He said nothing but we knew he had found it, for we saw him kneel suddenly before it as if his legs had given out, and his eyes had teared up significantly by the time we caught up to him. Rami and I, unsure of what to do or say, simply knelt on either side of him; each of us placing a hand upon his shoulder as he buried his face in his own rugged hands and began to weep.

After a while we stood and stepped away, allowing him some time to grieve alone. As we sat on a nearby wooden bench, listening to the birds cast their vivacious songs into the mournful breeze, I watched Leo remove his necklace – a silver crucifix – and place it gently on his mother's marker. He looked over at us then and seemed surprised to see us, as if he'd once again forgotten that we were there.

"Would you mind if I hang out here for the rest of the day?" he asked with a pained smile.

"Of course not," I said. "We'll come and reclaim you before nightfall."

:: Posting #55 ::

Divergent Tributaries

We returned, as promised, just before sunset.

From the distance, as we exited the RV, we could see him standing in nearly the same spot where we had left him. Only now he wasn't alone: a silver-haired man in a white robe stood alongside him, and for a moment I couldn't help wondering whether he'd conjured up a ghost.

The man appeared to hand something to Leo and then turned and walked away. By the time we reached the gravesite the mysterious figure had already entered a pickup truck and driven away, in a very non-ghostlike manner, and I deduced that Leo had already made himself a new friend in the form of the church's reverend.

It was also evident that he'd been tending with great diligence to his mother's grave, for the leaves and debris had been cleared from all about it, and he had adorned the simple marker with an abundance of wildflowers which he'd probably garnered with patient effort from the surrounding fields.

He seemed genuinely excited to see us, and his familiar smile had returned to some extent.

"Hey, guys, guess what happened?"

I failed on all three guesses, the last one being that a songbird had flown over and deposited an unwanted gift upon his shabby head.

"No," he said, though at least I had drawn a chuckle.

He proceeded to show us a dull, bronze-colored key which he had pulled from a back pocket.

"I hope that's not a key to a brand-new mausoleum you're planning on moving into," I ventured.

He laughed again and waved his hand at me dismissively.

"Wrong again. It's a key to the rear entrance to the church's cellar, where I'll be staying for the next few weeks."

He'd met the minister, he explained, who had spotted him sitting alone in the graveyard and had come out to greet him – the same man whom we had observed when we drove up.

"He knew my mother," he added excitedly, "and he plans on returning tomorrow so he can fill me in on more of what he remembers about her."

Further, the kindly old priest, upon discovering that Leo was homeless, had insisted he take up residence for as long as he wished in the church's basement, where there was a small guestroom that was seldom used.

"He told me that my mother was a kindly old woman, and that this is what she would have wanted. She spoke of me often, he said, so it seems we have a lot to talk about. I don't know how long I'll be here, but I feel it's where I need to stay for now. I plan on earning my keep as security guard and groundskeeper in the meantime," he added proudly.

"You'll make an excellent living scarecrow," I assured him. "If I were thinking of breaking into the church to steal – what would I steal? the holy chalice, let's say – and I spotted you haunting its graveyard, I'd high-tail it on out of here for sure."

I was glad he could appreciate my childish humor.

"I'll really miss you guys," he said, "and I appreciate your bringing me out here to find my mother." (He spoke as if she were still alive.) "I truly hope our paths will cross again, somewhere downriver. Meanwhile, there's a beautiful city in Brazil – named after a river, appropriately enough – that's awaiting your visit, I do believe."

So, this was where our overlapping journeys would end, it appeared; the point where our lives would move along on their separate tributaries. But I was glad they had intersected for at least a little while.

I couldn't help trying to force some funds on him just one more time – again to no avail. He had what provisions he needed, he insisted, and would take not a penny more. He did, however, accept a big hug from me, and an even bigger one (unavoidably) from Rami.

He returned his attention to his mother as we turned and walked away.

I looked back at him for a moment, from the edge of the graveyard. In my mind I still see him there, his guitar case slung between his shoulders; speaking softly to his departed mother and fussing over her grave, as the wind continued to sigh and the birds continued to sing and life continued on, unwilling to wait on those who remain behind to tend to the ones who have fallen.

I consoled myself with the thought that he was used to taking care of himself, and fortunately there were still a handful of benevolent souls, like the kindly old priest whom we saw but never met, who were willing to lend an eye – and a hand – as well. He'd return to Pennsylvania in his own good time, I presumed; perhaps repeating his original pilgrimage along those endless railroad tracks.

I had paths of my own I needed to follow, but there could be no doubt that I would miss him.

:: Posting #56 ::

Detour

I must apologize to my social media followers – the number of which has grown beyond my wildest expectations, judging by the number of "likes" and comments received on my previous postings – for my uncustomary silence. Much has happened of late which has distracted me from my writing; some of which I shall have great difficulty expressing. Nevertheless, I believe my loyal readers deserve to learn the outcome of my quest.

For yes, my journey has ended, you see – though not in the way I might have wished or expected. But, as eager as I am to end this narrative, I mustn't get ahead of myself. "Slow down," I must tell myself (as I often say to Rami), "and enjoy the scenery."

I'll begin by saying we never made it to Brazil.

After leaving our beloved Leo at his new – and no doubt temporary – abode in Massachusetts, Rami and I began navigating back to our own home base in Cape May, meaning to begin preparations for our international excursion. (Jacob, I figured, being the most apt to aid us in this endeavor.)

Since we weren't on any sort of schedule or pressing timetable, we decided to make a pitstop in Atlantic City – the enticingly misnomered "Jewel of the Atlantic" – to see what all the hoopla was about.

Well, to be more factual, Rami had already been there a couple of times before, whereas if I had ever been, I certainly didn't remember it – which was nothing new for me. In any event, we both agreed we could do with a little rest and recreation.

It was amusing right off the bat, I must admit, as we pulled into the ornate covered entrance of a prestigious gambling resort, to see the look on the valet's face when Rami tossed him the key to our RV so he could find someplace to park it. (The sign for 'valet parking', after all, did not specify any restrictions.)

"Help yourself to one of the tasty-cakes in the kitchen cabinet," offered Rami in lieu of a tip.

"I hope you got a receipt for that," I said to him.

"You mean the tasty-cakes?"

"No, I was thinking more in terms of our million-dollar RV." (I was becoming ever less trustful of people, I'm sad to say, after learning how even our homeless friend had been robbed.) "If we're going to give that thing away, I'd much rather gift it to someone like Leo."

"Don't worry, Boss, he gave me a parking voucher. Besides, believe it or not, these guys are used to parking vehicles even more expensive than ours."

As if to give credence to his claim, a gleaming, gold-colored Rolls Royce came gliding into the portico. Two valets rushed out – one to either side of the vehicle – and held open the respective doors. From the driver's side emerged a well-groomed, silver-haired man dressed to the nines in a white tuxedo, bright red bow tie and white fedora. From the passenger's side stepped out an eye-catching blond dressed all in black. She was bedazzled in diamonds and displayed a rather generous portion of her shapely legs, and appeared to be a third of the age of her distinguished partner.

The elderly man, who had left the car running, handed his valet a crisp banknote which appeared to contain multiple zeros as he converged toward his blond, offered her his elbow, and escorted her inside. She nuzzled coquettishly against him while two additional valets held open the automatic doors. Not one of the attendants had seemed all that impressed with the Rolls Royce, but none could seem to take their eyes off the blond.

Teasingly, I winged my elbow toward Rami, but he just shook his head and preceded me inside.

As we stepped into the casino's grand atrium, I was awed by all the crystal and marble and life-sized statues and flowing glass fountains and glittering lights and the myriads of flowers and plants and even actual trees by which it was ornamented. It was a bit overwhelming to the senses, without a doubt - as was the cumbersomeness of that previous sentence to my sensible readers, I wouldn't doubt. My point being, all the gold and the glitter and the fine adornments made me feel a tad underdressed in my ragged jeans and plain white t-shirt.

"Perhaps we should have stopped at a fashion store before coming here," I said to Rami, who, aside from a leather cap and a bomber's jacket, wasn't dressed any fancier than I.

"There's plenty of them inside," he assured me. "Besides, around here they don't judge you so much by the quality of your attire as by the robustness of your bankroll, so you should be just fine."

We ascended toward the gaming area in a centrally located, extra elongated escalator, the sides of which were of crystal-clear glass permitting an open view of the expansive atrium; the whole of it brightly illuminated by grand, overhanging chandeliers. As we neared the top, I could tell festivities were in full swing, as the cacophony of mechanical clicks and bells, intermingling with the conversations and cheers of the crowd, swelled to an almost overbearing degree.

"Well, these people certainly seem to be enjoying distributing their bankrolls," I said.

"That's the name of the game here, Boss. People pretending they have money to burn and that they don't mind doing so — all for the potential thrill of hitting the big one. Trust me, though, none of them actually enjoy losing — which is what the vast majority wind up doing."

"Well then, we may as well join the crowd. What's my allowance, by the way?"

"It's your money, Boss. So long as we leave here with enough to refuel the RV, it's none of my concern. Personally, I don't intend to spend any more than a day's pay."

"Okay, but I can spot you a lot more than that if you need me to. We should do our best to support the local economy."

Rami led us to one of the high-rollers tables within a slightly less crowed section of the casino, where he took a seat and purchased a small stack of chips. I stood behind and watched him play a few hands of poker — which he proved once again to be pretty good at, judging by his steadily growing pile of multicolored tokens. After a while, as it became obvious that he wasn't going to need my help, I wished him luck and told him I was going to stroll about for a bit.

"Okay; just don't get too carried away. You can burn through money a lot quicker than you might think, especially at this end of the casino" he admonished.

"Don't worry," I lied (for I had a thick roll of hundred's burning my pocket), "I only plan on window-shopping."

I wandered over to a sectioned-off area of slot machines, attracted by all the bells and whistles. I decided to be frugal and begin on one with the lowest cost, which was a mere five dollars a pull (figuring Rami would be proud of me). I became instantly addicted, of course, quickly losing track of both my time and my money.

Try as I might, however (for I really wanted to become part of the "in" crowd), I just couldn't seem to shrink my bankroll. Seems I was particularly lucky with the sevens: one hundred dollars here, five hundred dollars there, and before I knew it, I had worked my way up to the $100 slots.

It was there that I noticed, just a couple of machines down from me, that same elderly man in the white tux, feeding a machine much like my own. His lovelier half stood watching from behind, one hand on his shoulder and the other nursing (simultaneously, somehow) a lit cigarette and a drink.

She caught me looking and I smiled and waved, and she tipped her glass to me as she smiled back – spilling a few drops of bright red liquid on the older man's suit. I grimaced exaggeratedly at this, and her smile broadened, while her man, oblivious to all, kept spinning the wheels on his sullenly silent machine.

I went back to pulling the lever on my own one-armed bandit, and my propensity for winning went on unabated. It was fun, I must admit, though I did feel a tad bit guilty. And the more my win-streak continued, as so brightly and loudly broadcast by my excitable machine, the more I attracted the attention of the sultry blonde. At last, she seemed unable to contain herself any longer and came sauntering over to admire my prowess – much to the stationary annoyance of her old man, who had finally taken notice of me. His lady appeared to cross the line however when she offered to buy me a drink (which I later learned were free to begin with), for he abandoned his losing machine and walked over to her, grabbed her by the arm and began dragging her away toward the roulette wheel. I waved and smiled once again as they looked back at me one more time, she with a smile and he with a scowl, just as my machine hit another jackpot – this one setting off literal sirens and flashing lights that encompassed the entire row of slot machines, including the one he'd just abandoned.

Rami came waltzing over just then, proudly displaying a fistful of $100 bills – though his enthusiasm shifted when he saw how many credits I had amassed on my machine, which was still flashing and blaring like a fire engine.

"Why is this thing carrying on so?" I asked, beginning to feel annoyed.

"Holy smokes, Boss, I think you just hit the progressive jackpot!"

"Is that a bad thing?"

"No, but I'm pretty sure it's going to require a tax form. An attendant should be stopping by with one any minute," he said, glancing about. "Maybe I should be the one to fill out that form, come to think of it: I don't think you'd want to attract the attention of the IRS, given your fake identity."

"Well, no need to get personal, but good thinking, Rami," I said, as we quickly switched places as if I'd been driving a stolen vehicle without a license – just before an attendant and a casino manager came striding over.

"Congratulations, young man," said the manager to Rami after verifying the winnings. "Would you mind if we take your picture?"

"I'd rather avoid any publicity," he replied.

"Understood."

Meanwhile the attendant, who evidently had been the one to fetch the manager when he's seen what had happened, glanced skeptically between me and Rami. (Perhaps he'd noticed the jail tattoo on Rami's shoulder, for he'd removed his bomber's jacket.)

"Are you sure you're the one who hit the jackpot, sir," he said to Rami, "and not the fellow who's standing behind you?"

"What? – oh, I see, because he's the white guy, I must not be the winner."

The attendant blushed, as the manager glared at him reprovingly.

"No, no, that's not what I meant at all. It's just – well, so long as you both agree on who won, that's all that matters."

"Yes," I vouched for Rami, "this is the man who will be paying all the taxes."

The thing being settled, Rami filled out the requisite paperwork and we were escorted to a private cashier for our payout. Rami chose cash over check or credit, and we waited and waited as they counted, recounted, and stacked all the bills. I even had time to hit the men's room.

"Don't worry, Boss," whispered Rami when I returned. He was juggling a load of wrapped $100 bills that was impressive even by my own jaded standards. "I'll hand these over to you when we get to our room."

"Room? Oh, you mean our RV."

"No, they comped us a luxury suite. The presidential one, if I'm not mistaken."

"Wow, they're definitely not sore losers. You mean we won all this cash, and they still felt compelled to give us something more?"

Rami declined an armed escort (he being his own best bodyguard), and they directed us toward the appropriate elevators. They even offered to fetch him a bag from the gift shop, which he declined as well.

"They're not being entirely unselfish," explained Rami after we'd begun walking. "They're hoping that, by keeping us here, we'll be tempted to spend back all this money."

"Well, we can certainly try," I offered.

We found our special elevator and ascended to the topmost floor, accessible via a special key by the elevator attendant.

"Looks like you had a pretty good run," said the man to Rami after some awkward silence. (Even the attendants were dressed far better than we, I couldn't help noticing.)

Rami nodded and dropped one of the packs of bills as the elevator lurched to a stop.

"Let the man keep that one," I said to Rami before he could stoop down. "It must be difficult riding up and down in this box all day long."

The man, seated on his silver bar stool, smiled broadly, thanked us profusely (with his Indian accent), then broke down crying.

"There, you see," I said as we walked down the plushily carpeted hallway, "we've begun giving it back already. Guy was a bit emotional, though, wouldn't you say?"

Rami nodded wordlessly, glancing at all the oil paintings and pedestals with naked statues interspersed between the rooms. Fancy mirrors adorned the ceiling, amplifying all the beauty.

Our room was a corner suite, at the furthermost end of the ornate hallway. It was the first hotel room I'd ever seen with a double-door entrance…let alone a doorbell.

Rami funneled the bundle of cash into my arms so he could retrieve the room key from his back pocket.

It was at this moment, as I was trying to balance the bundles of Benjamins, that a familiar couple came walking down the hallway in our direction. It was none other than the stylish and stuffy old man and his stunning companion, of course, returning from the casino floor empty-handed. As they pulled up to the (single-doored) room just precedent to our own, the lady flashed me another beguiling smile after sizing up my wad.

"Nice six-pack you have there, young man" she said coyly.

The man in the wine-speckled white suit merely glared at me contemptuously, snatched up his lady and shuffled her inside, slamming the door behind them.

"Not all is well in the honeymoon suite tonight, I don't imagine" I said to Rami as he pushed open our doors and we stepped into our own.

The presidential suite proved lavish indeed, to put it mildly. It boasted wall to wall, floor to ceiling windows in every room, an oversized, wrap-around balcony that fronted the ocean, and an enormous bathroom with marble floor and gold fixtures and a jacuzzi tub the size of a small swimming pool, just for starters. There were two lush bedrooms, either of which could have served as the master, a full-sized, fully furnished living room with large-screen TV, and a dining room with a cherry wood table that could have easily accommodate King Arthur and all his merry men. (And I may have mixed my literary metaphors there; perhaps I should have said it could easily have seated all the participants in the Last Supper while providing for a very fine da Vinci oil-painting to boot.) There was also a full-sized kitchen, of course, which communicated with the dining room by way of a breakfast bar equipped with chrome, leather-topped stools.

"So, what do you think, Rami?" I asked as we stood at the railing of the balcony enjoying the view of the ocean and the melancholic crying of the seagulls. "Not too shabby, eh? Nearly comparable to the comforts of our RV."

"Yes," he said, "and that's what has me worried."

"What do you mean?"

"Well, when your luck runs this good, you have to wonder when the other shoe is going to drop."

"I have no idea what that even means, Rami. But speaking of shoes, I suppose, if we're staying here overnight, we should go and fetch some more things."

"Sure," he said. "We'll just have to find out where they parked our RV."

"Nah, I was thinking of visiting one of the casino's boutiques: I was impressed by some of the things I saw in the windows. If we're going to mingle another day with the other high rollers, we may as well dress the part. I was a little jealous of that older man's suit, to be honest."

"Are you sure it was his suit and not his lady friend?"

"Ah, you called my bluff on that one, Rami. I suppose that's why you're such a good poker player."

"Be that as it may, I should warn you that shopping at one of those boutiques is going to put a nice dent in your newly-won fortune."

I shrugged my shoulders.

"No worries. To borrow another of your pithy sayings, 'Easy come, easy go.' Besides, you could do with some new threads yourself – if nothing more than a nice silk pair of pajamas. I've seen that old jail-suit you keep wearing at night: it's getting pretty threadbare."

"Very well, Boss, if you insist. Just give me a minute to stash your cash in the room safe."

"Okay. But leave out a bundle or two for us to take along."

A little while later, as we were riding back down the elevator (which had been set back to automatic, the attendant's stool no longer occupied), it occurred to me to ask: "So tell me some more about that shoe."

"The sh--? Oh, right. It's something my mother used to say, implying that things usually happen in twos. More specifically, she believed that every stroke of luck, be it good or bad, is paired with its opposite. I might also have used the metaphor of the pendulum, which can only swing one way for so long before it comes swinging back."

Turned out his mother was right: for on the very next morning the other shoe fell, and was struck by the back-swinging pendulum.

:: Posting #57 ::

Contact

Though we each had our own sprawling bedroom and the king-sized beds (which could easily have slept king Arthur and all his well-fed disciples, to abuse an analogy) were extraordinarily comfortable, we both rose early on the following day.

I ordered a lavish room-service breakfast which, though delivered to our troop-sized table, we wound up enjoying on the balcony, as the sun arose out of the ocean.

Though a familiar spectacle, it was one I never tired of witnessing: each sunrise casting a slightly different interplay of light and color between sky and sea.   Certain distinctive memories - something I have learned to cherish - are attached to them as well, going back to that very first morning I awoke in a hotel room in Cape May with no recollection of anything that had come before. On this occasion, however, my mind drifted back to Melanie; to that golden evening when we sat holding hands in her gazebo, enjoying an unusual sunset off the western shores of the Florida Keys.

But back to that other shoe.

My drifting thoughts led eventually to Esmeralda, and I figured I ought to give her a call, to warn her that Rami and I were home-bound (remembering my adoptive mother's affectionate displeasure the last time we surprised her). I told Rami as much, as he began gathering up our empty plates.

"Good thinking, Boss. That way she'll have one of her awesome, home-cooked meals awaiting us."

"I swear, Rami, you have a one-track mind."

"Only when there aren't any women around," he countered.

"Ah, so maybe I'm not the only one who's coveting our neighbor's wife."

"Nah, she's not my type."

"I see," I said, nodding skeptically.

I'd seen the types that caught his darting eyes, and she looked pretty much like most of them. But I decided to let it pass.

I went inside to the leather sofa and dialed my Cape May home. Esmeralda picked up halfway through the first ring.

"Hello, mother dear, just thought I'd call to – "

"John, is this you?" she interjected, sounding even more excitable than usual.

"Yes. Sorry I haven't called you in a while, we've – "

"John, thank God you called!"

"What is it, Esmeralda, is everything alright?"

"Your father called; he's been trying to get ahold of you."

:: Posting #58 ::

If the Shoe Fits

"My – who did you say called?" I stammered into the phone.

"Your father. I'm afraid he isn't doing so well, John. He really wants to talk to you."

I felt my ears going numb.

"My father … Did he say where he was calling from?"

She gave me the address and number to a hospital in Houston and I hung up the phone; my mind reeling as I cradled the receiver. Could this truly be my father, I asked myself, or could it be just some prankster trying to tap me for a loan? (I'd revealed perhaps a bit too much of myself on social media, after all, including the phone number to my house in Cape May.) But something about this sounded genuine – the apparent desperation, perhaps, with which this man was trying to reach me? Yet I was equally desperate to find my parents so I should proceed with some healthy skepticism, I cautioned myself.

Nevertheless my hands were shaking as I retrieved the phone and dialed the number.

"Hello?" a female voice responded.

"Hi, this is … John. I'm trying to reach -- is my father there?" I asked, feeling slightly ridiculous.

"You're James' son?" the pleasant voice asked.

"I … yes," I ventured. "Yes, I am. And to whom might I be speaking?"

"I'm his nurse."

(A slight pause.)

"I'm sorry, sir, but your father can't speak to you just now. He's – he's not feeling so well."

(I recall our conversation word for word.)

"What's wrong with him?" I asked, feeling deeply concerned about this man whom, for all I knew, I'd never even met.

"I can't really tell you too much over the phone," she said gently, "but I'd advise you to come visit as soon as possible. As soon as you can safely get here, I should add."

I'd be there just as soon as I could catch a plane, I assured her; looking out the window as if expecting to see one hovering nearby. My entire body was now numb as I set down the receiver, missing the cradle by a fair margin.

Rami, who'd caught part of my conversation with the nurse, appeared to sense my distress.

"You okay, Boss?" he asked, sitting down on the sofa beside me.

I filled him in on what I'd learned, and he immediately sprang to action.

"Don't you worry, Boss; I'll get you to Houston," he assured me.

In a matter of minutes, he'd booked us a flight.

I called the front desk and reserved our room through the remainder of the week (so we wouldn't have to worry about moving the RV) and within a half-hour more we were in a cab on the way to the airport.

:: Posting #59 ::

An Abbreviated Reunion

The flight to Texas felt interminable. Rami and I spoke little, for it seemed pointless to speculate on what time would soon reveal. I do vaguely recall some blond-haired stewardess who appeared to be hitting on Rami, for she kept delivering cordials to his first-class seat…not one of which he ever consumed but kept passing them off to me. (As you can imagine, I was feeling pretty braced by the time we landed.)

Much more vivid is the memory of arriving via cab at the Houston Methodist Hospital, riding up an elevator that reeked of sanitizer, exiting into a brightly lit, whitewashed hallway, and then stepping up to a bustling nurses' station.

We were greeted by a nurse (I'll call her Lori) whose voice I immediately recognized.

"Wow, you did arrive pretty quickly" she said after we'd introduced ourselves. "I was hoping you'd get here before my shift ended but I wasn't truly counting on it."

She took me by the arm and began escorting Rami and me to my (presumed) father's room, down a hallway that appeared endlessly lengthened as if by a trick of reciprocating mirrors.

"I don't know how your father looked the last you saw him" she gently warned, not knowing that neither did I, "but he's probably looking much rougher than how you last remember."

She briefly explained to me, as we proceeded down the endless corridor, how he was suffering from complications of Malaria, on top of newly diagnosed metastatic cancer. None of it sounded very promising, but I appreciated her candor.

"He's been having trouble staying awake, let alone eating or drinking" she concluded, as we paused at last outside an open doorway. I could feel the hairs on my arms standing on end.

"Do you want me to come in with you?" she asked considerately.

"No, I'll be fine; my friend will stay with me" I said, with an appreciative glance at Rami.

Right before entering the room, I had a brief, urine-stained flashback of our ill-fated visit to Stew in that hospital in Key West, and I hoped the present experience would not unfold in any way similar – though I probably could have done with the comedic relief.

As we stepped inside, I saw that a privacy curtain had been drawn around his bed – though I wasn't sure why, as it was a single room. The man's appearance must be off-putting indeed, I assumed. I walked slowly toward the shrouded bed, as Rami made his way to a nearby recliner.

"I'll be right here if you need me, Boss" he said, and I knew he was affording me some privacy.

I slipped behind the curtain and was stunned to see an older me lying in the bed.

His eyes were closed, and he was apparently sleeping. Though his face was emaciated and gaunt, I knew in an instant that this was my father – whether in part from veiled memories I couldn't be certain.

Tremulously, tentatively, I touched the gnarled, thick-veined hand that lay overtop the bedsheet.

A flicker of eyelids, but the eyes remained shut.

It occurred to me suddenly that I didn't know what to call him.

"Hey, old man" I opted softly.

This time the eyes opened slightly – then widened with evident surprise and amazement.

"James!" he rasped weakly.

(So I hadn't been all that far off in my choice of names…)

"Hello, Dad."

It felt odd enunciating those two simple words.

"So it's really you – you really came!" he whispered. "Unless this is another of my feverish dreams."

"If it is, Dad, then we're sharing the same one."

There was so much that flooded through my mind just then; so much I wanted to ask him – beginning with how he'd tracked me down – but I could see he was weak and had difficulty speaking. His lips were parched and dry, as if he'd been traveling the desert for forty days.

"Is… is mother okay?" I finally ventured to ask.

His brow became more furrowed than before.

"I don't know," he said simply; and I could see the sudden hurt in his eyes which my words had evoked.

"I'm sorry, Dad. It's just that, now that I've finally found you, I was hoping I might find her as well. Complete the reunion, so to speak. There's so much that I've forgotten, you see. So much I don't understand."

"No!" he said abruptly, emphatically, with as much force as he could seem to muster. "You mustn't look for her – promise me you won't!"

I wasn't quite sure how to respond.

"Promise me," he insisted, and there was desperation in his tone.

I nodded my head just to appease him, and he relaxed a bit.

"Besides, she's changed her name and her location, and she's carefully guarded. You'd never come near her - and it would be far too dangerous for you to try."

Another pause, as he drew a deep breath. He must have seen the italicized question mark in my eyes.

"You're supposed to be dead, you see."

A shiver ran up my spine as a small piece of the chaotic puzzle fell into place. So many more lay scattered around and disconnected, however.

"Okay, but I need to know what happened, at least. Can you at least give me a couple of clues?"

Instead, he smiled at me, and his face fully relaxed.

"It's so good to see you again, my son," he said as he squeezed my hand.

He looked so peaceful as he closed his eyes … and never opened them again.

:: Posting #60 ::

A Funeral and a Friend

His nurse actually came to the funeral.

"There's some things I wanted to tell you at the hospital," she said to me afterward, "but my shift had ended, and I needed to pick up my kids. I'm also truly sorry I wasn't with him, or the two of you, when he passed."

I waved it off.

"Thanks for coming to the funeral," I said sincerely; my eyes still watery from watching the casket being lowered. "You boosted the attendance by almost fifty percent!"

She smiled at this – a smile that was a genuine part of her therapeutic arsenal, without a doubt.

"Something in your eyes, just before I left, told me you still had a lot of unanswered questions, and I felt compelled to come see you. There's a couple of things I can probably clear up for you. Besides, I had grown quite fond of your old man: he was a kind, if rather silent, patient."

"I am eager to hear anything you have to share with me," I assured her.

We made our way to a bench underneath a tree, where she sat herself down between me and Rami and began to talk.

She explained, first of all, how my father had been flown up from a hospital in Manaus, the capital city of the Brazilian Amazon, as his infirmities had become too complex for them to treat.

"He did well at first, under the concerted care of an oncologist and a disease specialist, but eventually – well, obviously – his illnesses got the best of him."

A squirrel looked us over, inquiringly, then scurried up the tree, surmising we had nothing to share with him.

"Did he ever say what he was doing in the Amazon?"

"He was a missionary and a philanthropist, as best I could gather. Tending to the bodies and souls of the indigenous tribes deep within the rainforest. That's about as much as I learned about that, however. He was, as I've said, rather silent and introspective. Certainly not one to talk or boast about himself."

I nodded (introspectively).

"How about ….my mother? Did he ever say anything about her?"

She appeared thoughtful for a while, as if trying to retrieve anything at all.

"No," she said finally, "not a single word. I'd gotten the distinct impression that he was separated or single, or at least working alone."

That seemed to make sense, given his work environment.

"Obviously he must have mentioned a son, however. What did he have to say about me?"

"To be completely honest, he thought you had been murdered."

"Then how on earth did he wind up finding me?"

"Ah, that's where I can shed some light. From your social media postings, believe it or not. You see, he was bored one day – it being one of his better days – and he asked me if I had anything good to read. (He wasn't too fond of television.) Well, I'm more of a TV than a book girl, I must admit, but I had stumbled across your blog postings not long ago, and it was the most interesting bit of reading I could think of. Besides, I thought he might find it fascinating as well, seeing as you both shared a propensity for traveling and helping others. I had no idea, of course, how much more than that you had in common, other than a presumed, coincidental resemblance.

"I began printing out your journal in stages on my home computer and bringing it to the hospital for him to read. He became instantly enthralled; almost addicted, it seemed. His eyes were growing steadily weaker, however, and it was becoming too tiresome for him to read, so I began reading it to him, piece by piece. It seemed to be the highlight of his days. In a matter of just a couple of weeks or so, we had read through your entire journal, up to the present."

"So, what made him decide that I was his son? The picture of myself that I had posted, I presume?"

"No; I only printed out the text, you see, not the pictures. (Call me frugal with my printer ink; it comes from being a single mother.) Evidently it was when you began talking about Brazil with that homeless man, and your mysterious understanding of Portuguese, that his mind was made up. It seems you used to live with him in Rio de Janeiro for a time, you see, before he travelled to the Amazon. Whether your mother was with you then, or whether either of you traveled with him to the rainforest, he did not say."

"And that was enough to convince him of who I was – and that I hadn't really died?"

"Well, partially that, but his hope had been ignited by something you posted early on – about that star-shaped mole on your butt cheek."

I'm sure I blushed at this, but it was all beginning to make sense.

"When he shared with me what he'd been suspecting," she went on, "what he'd been hoping for against all hope, I remembered about that picture of yourself which you had posted. He begged me to print it out and bring it in - which is what I had already planned on doing. I came back with it that same evening, in fact, after work. Well, that was the clincher, of course: he took one look at it and began to cry."

We spent a good while talking after that, but there wasn't a whole lot more she could add to my mysterious story. The afternoon shadows were lengthening, and we all had places we needed to be. (It seems the only funeral that can truly bring life to a complete halt will be our own.)

"I'm so sorry you didn't get more of the answers you've been seeking," she said as we stood up. "And I'm especially sorry that you lost your father so soon after finding him. If it's of any comfort, I know it meant the world to him to discover you were still alive, and to see you one more time before passing. I think that's the only reason he held on as long as he did."

"I appreciate all you did for him," I said earnestly. "My own path forward has been laid out more clearly now: I have plenty of clues to get me started if I'm to find my mother and resolve what truly happened. And I'm hoping this meeting with my father will stir some more of those latent memories, despite the brevity of our reunion. One thing is certain: none of it would have happened if not for you."

She smiled appreciatively.

"I've really enjoyed following your story, but I never imagined I'd become a part of it. I can't wait to read the ending – I truly hope it's happily ever after."

We all hugged again and a few more tears were shed as we parted ways – though not before I had coaxed her into giving me her address. I told her I just wanted to keep in touch, but I'll apologize to her now (if she is reading this) for telling only half the truth. I had an ulterior motive, of course, which I'm sure she figured out long before this confession.

Let's just say I figured out what to do with the remaining cash from the casino.

And something tells me she'll be placing flowers on my father's grave from time to time, in my absence.

Back Where It All Began

(Never Posted)

The preceding turned out to be my final posting on social media. In view of what I've since discovered, I thought it best to delete my journal and close my account altogether. My faithful followers will be angry or disappointed, I should imagine, but I must let them think what they will – hopefully they'll simply write me off as a phony, a talentless purveyor of false tales. But I've decided it's in the best interest of everyone involved, including myself.

Still, I will privately save and complete this journal, and set it aside as future testament. If you are reading this now, then no one involved can be harmed any longer by my disclosure.

Picking up, therefore, on where I left off:

I thought I'd been holding up rather well, all things considered; but it wasn't until we'd picked up our RV in Atlantic City and were headed back home to Cape May that it all began to sink in.

I'd found my father.

I'd lost my father.

I'd learned my real name, that much was true; but I still didn't know who I really was [had been], nor what had truly happened to me.

And why had my father urged me so fervently to never seek my mother? Was she my would-be murderess? Or was there some other secret he didn't want me to know?

Well, I was determined to find out, even if it killed me.

I brooded upon these things for most of the way home; and the more I brooded, the stronger grew my determination: the more eager I became to complete my quest, once and for all.

It was to this end that I channeled all my emotion and sorrow: the time for abject grief and mourning would have to wait just a little bit longer.

Or so I thought…

It felt good to reunite with Esmeralda and the rest of my adoptive family, to be sure. They greeted Rami and me as if they hadn't seen us in ages, though we really hadn't been gone all that long on this occasion. They did their best to comfort me, of course, when they learned about my father; but somehow, the abundance of love that flowed through and among this precious family only seemed to accentuate the very thing that I had lost.

All that physically remained of my father was a small leather pouch which the hospital had bequeathed me, containing nothing more than a thin black wallet, and his passport. (Evidently my father, like Leo, was a man who traveled light.) I doubted there was much more he'd left behind in the Brazilian jungle, aside from his heart and soul - his love for the people unto whom he ministered. I hoped to travel there myself one day - perhaps with Rami if he'd be willing - but for now I had a more pressing agenda.

My inheritance would seem meager to most, but to me it was priceless. My father's passport was the master key to unlocking my past, and I intended to begin my research the very next day at the local library.

I'm sure I seemed broody throughout dinner, despite the magnificence of the feast which Esmeralda had prepared for us and the cheerful banter with which I was surrounded. Afterward, as Rami remained downstairs to help with the cleanup (at the children's cajoling, who were always quite eager to hear his embellished stories), I made my way to my preferred bedroom in the upper garrets, craving some time to myself. And for the first time since I'd found (and lost) my father, I began to weep; a flood of tears that I thought would never cease. But eventually they did, as my sorrow turned slowly to anger, and then ultimately to rage. I felt frustrated with the whole situation, with the apparent futility of it all – including my father's nagging plea that I never seek out my mother. And all at once I experienced a complete reversal of my feelings and desires. Suddenly, I just wanted to be done with it all: to honor my father's death wish, abandon my pointless quest and allow the past to remain buried, along with my beloved father.

I remembered the leather bag that had contained the sum of my possessions when I'd awakened, with no memories, in that nearby hotel room (now seemingly a lifetime ago), and it became the focal point of my rage. I retrieved the bag from my closet, where it had lain empty and neglected for so long, and I began ripping it to shreds with my pocket-knife; trying to destroy once and for all this symbolic link to my forgotten past.

As I tore through its fabric I discovered, tucked between the inner lining and the reinforced base of the bag, an envelope that had been secreted there all the while, completely unsuspected. I had sliced it nearly in half, in fact, before I even noticed it. Curiosity temporarily quelled my rage, and I set down my pocketknife.:

I opened the envelope to discover a letter, typed in very small font - presumably so that more words would fit onto its pages.

In an ironic stroke of fate, it proved to be a letter from my mother.

A Letter from the Past

"*My Dearest James,*" the letter began.

"*Due to the sensitivity of its contents I plan to sew this letter into the lining of your bag, which is where I trust you've found it. (I can't risk having it fall into the wrong hands between the time of my writing it and the time you receive it, as you will come to understand.) I'll instruct your would-be executioner to tell you where it is not long before he knocks you out, that the memory of it may be fresh when you awaken.*"

[Well, *that* plan sure did fail…]

"*I must also apologize in advance for what is likely to be a very long missive; but this will be, of necessity, my final communication with you, and I have a lot of things I'd like to explain.*

"*First of all, I sincerely hope, as you're reading this, that Sayyid didn't harm you too badly.*"

[Strike two, I'm out.]

"*Trust me, though, the alternative would have been far worse. My husband demanded a photograph of you lying seriously wounded and bleeding on the deck, you see, just before Sayyid was to toss you overboard, so it had to appear convincing. It was also important for you to grasp the precariousness of your position, though I regret that the point had to be emphasized in such a painful manner.*

"*Turns out my husband is a far more jealous man than I ever could have imagined – and I spare you from referring to him as your stepdad, for I know he never lived up to such a title. I thought he'd remain content to simply ignore you while devoting all his affection towards me; but the older you became, the more you reminded him of your father (for the resemblance is truly uncanny), and he became ever more mindful and resentful of your existence. To add to his bitterness, he and I were unable to bear children together, and I believe it rankled him to no end to think you might become his sole inheritor.*

"As it turns out, I have given you your inheritance early, as you can see, in the form of my own endowment. It pains me to part with it, to be honest (especially those magnificent stones), but I want to facilitate your new beginning. Beyond that, I hope my gift helps prove to you how much I truly love you.

"Admittedly, as you're aware, there's plenty more wealth where that came from: I have only to pout or bat an eye at him to be given my heart's desire. When it comes to you, however, it has proven to be a different story: he has no qualms in taking you away from me, it seems, under the guise of a fatal accident – no doubt believing he can soothe my subsequent grief through an unending abundance of luxury and riches. While I confess to having a weakness for such things, I'd never want you to think I wouldn't give it all up if I could just have you back with me again.

"In any event, it was his growing jealousy and resentment towards you, I am sure, that led to his murderous scheme. He ordered his right-hand man to take you to America on another business and recreational trip; only this time you were to fall victim to a fatal boating accident. If you check the local newspaper, in fact, you're likely to read about your own alleged drowning: for Sayyid was supposed to report it as such after safely sequestering you in a local hotel room. I can almost envision the headline: 'Wealthy Arabian Emir's stepson falls off boat while pleasure-sailing and is feared drowned' – or something to that effect. (And I'm sure Sayyid will bring my husband a clipping of the article as further proof that he completed his task.)

"There'll be no photograph of you to accompany the article, of course, for no such images exist: it was out of shame for your existence that my husband kept you from the limelight. You were like his best-kept, dirty little secret. (He keeps me carefully secluded and hidden as well, for that matter; but I believe, in my case, this is due to his extreme possessiveness.) Regardless, this anonymity will factor in your favor as you begin your new life in America, for no one will recognize you for who you truly are. Still, you should probably lay low for a while, and avoid publicity as much as possible going forward. Some cosmetic and fashion changes may not hurt as well, for no one – especially my husband – must ever discover that you're still alive.

"Meanwhile, you must be wondering how I uncovered my husband's plot (if you haven't figured it out already). Well, while normally so shrewd, what he failed to perceive was Sayyid's intense fondness of you...not to mention myself. Sayyid came to see himself as a surrogate father to you throughout your own father's absence and my husband's neglect - and I could tell, by your interactions, that you returned his

affection. Fortunately for you and me, therefore, Sayyid informed me beforehand of my husband's intent, and we devised our own counterplan for your fake demise – knowing full well that, if Sayyid didn't at least appear to carry out my husband's demands, he'd merely find someone else to do so; no doubt dispensing with Sayyid in the process. There's simply no swaying him once he's made up his mind about something - which is probably how he came to be so powerful and rich, and how I became added to his coveted possessions.

"For the sake of full disclosure, what my husband has also failed to recognize is that my feelings for Sayyid run far deeper than friendship, or the affinity of a mistress toward her loyal servant. I've become completely enamored by him, truth be told, and my feelings are fully reciprocated; but this is another thing my husband must never know. We could try and elope, of course, but we both know he'd simply track us down like the exotic game he loves to illegally hunt and kill in the Amazon.

"Yes, it's a very tangled web that I have woven. Please don't worry for me, though: I assure you I'm doing fine. Sayyid and I have grown accustomed to all the perks and luxuries my husband provides, and the inherent danger in continuing our tryst beneath his blind watch keeps the excitement very much alive.

"So there you have it, my son; I've come 'clean' with you, as it were, by exposing all my dirt. I don't imagine you've ever thought too highly of me anyway, beginning with the day I left – and took you from - your father.

"Ironically, though, it is my dalliance that has ultimately saved your life, for I know I can trust Sayyid to deliver on his promises. I'm certain he'll make it appear as though you died, while secretly depositing you in a safe location along with your bag of riches.

"The amount should be sufficient to sustain you in your new life, I should think – and I strongly suggest that you begin one. Forget the old you as much as possible, in other words: you should adopt an entirely new identity. For this reason, any cards or documents containing your real ID will have been carefully removed from your possession, so you'll need to procure some new ones.

"As it turns out, Sayyid happens to know (from my husband's former 'business' dealings) of someone who can help you obtain such documents. He happens to be the manager of the very hotel in which you'll be staying. This manager has absolutely no knowledge of our plan nor even of who you are; but you should have no difficulty striking a deal with him on your own, for Sayyid assures me he can be bribed for a fair price. (He's not a dishonest man per se, he informs me, he's just unafraid

to bend the rules.) Sayyid and I have tried to think of everything we could, you see, to ease your transition.

"Additionally, it is crucial that you never attempt to contact me again in any way nor for any reason, for it wouldn't just be your own life that you'd be risking. Trust me, should my husband find out that you were spared, he'd probably finish you off himself, then dispose of Sayyid (and probably myself) in the process, upon learning of his betrayal.

"Likewise, for the safety of everyone involved, I would strongly discourage you from trying to reach your father. To ensure that your death appears absolutely convincing, Sayyid plans on tracking down your father during his upcoming mercenary trip to the Amazon, to inform him of your unfortunate drowning. Your father will probably suspect foul play, but there'll be nothing he can do about it; and at least his grief and anger will seem quite real should he and my husband's paths ever intersect again. (They frequent the jungle for different reasons: my husband for illegal hunting and the extortion of gold and jewels from local miners, whereas your father prefers to mine for souls; but occasionally their paths still meet.)

"The news of your untimely death will sorely grieve your father, I know (and undeservedly so), but I also know that his work will sustain him. He has proven to me that his love for the indigenous tribes of the jungle supersedes all other desires, including those he once felt towards me. He's as obsessed, in that respect, as my current husband is with his riches.

"If it counts for anything, I have always considered your father to be a very good man - far better than I ever deserved. When I told him I was leaving him for my wealthy Arabian suitor, for instance, he did not fight me nor even disparage me. 'If that's what it takes to make you happy' is pretty much all he said. He did try and fight me, however - quite vehemently, in fact - when I told him I meant to take you with me. Ultimately, I convinced him that it was for your own good; that we could give you a much better life and education than you could ever receive in the savage rain forest, where you'd more likely die of malaria or some similar disease or be slain by some wild beast or naked savage. This appeal for your safety and well-being is what ultimately swayed him, for I know he always had your best interest at heart.

I should have told you all this much sooner, I realize, for I think it's important for you to know that it wasn't for lack of loving you that he let you go. In truth, he is the most unselfish person I have ever known; far beyond anything I could ever pretend to be. I didn't mind being with him so much when we lived in the beautiful city of Rio, which I know you loved as well; but the move to the Amazon jungle, while perhaps seeming *like an exotic adventure to you, was a stark change I couldn't for long endure. I'm simply not endowed with your father's self-sacrificing nature, you see; hence my susceptibility to the 'Arabian Prince' (as he seemed to me then). He appeared to fall for me at first sight upon wandering into one of the villages where your father was ministering. He made a point to stop by our village on a regular basis after that (which happened to be in proximity to a goldmining site he'd been exploiting), and it wasn't long before I'd fallen for his charisma and charm. That, combined with the allure of leaving the bug-infested forest for a much more comfortable and lavish lifestyle, proved to be a temptation I couldn't resist. He was tall, rugged, mysterious, and handsome, whereas I was still relatively young, beautiful, gullible, and naïve, and he wound up being my 'knight in shining armor' who rescued me from my misery and despair. I convinced myself I was rescuing you as well, though in the end I have wound up placing you in a situation of even greater danger.*

"Even so, my son, I hope your story, much like my own, will have its happy ending.

"I'm sorry for not having included any of your personal items in the bag, but you really do need to make a clean break. Besides, like your father, you were never one to amass material things. Which was just as well, for my husband was never one to provide you with any. I do plan on including a small assortment of your favorite pictures (excluding those of any persons, of course) knowing how you enjoyed taking photographs of nature. Most of which you took during your many business trips with Sayyid, as I recall - which my husband was only ever too eager to send you on, to get you out of his sight.

"I hope your new life's journey takes you to many more places of profound beauty, that you may add abundantly to your collection.

"Finally, I'll not pretend to have been a good mother, any more than I have been (or shall ever be) a good and faithful wife. But please believe me when I say that I have always loved you, in my own selfish and distorted way. The best I can wish for you is that you will find someone who will love you in the way that you deserve, which is far more perfectly than I was able.

"Though forever absent, I shall evermore remain
      Your devoted mother."

Full Circle

Well, if my emotions had been on a roller-coaster ride before, the cart flew completely off the rails after reading this unsavory letter.

Mostly what I felt, after reading her rambling words, was a profound sense of sadness, betrayal, and confusion. I didn't quite know whether to laugh, to scream or to cry.

She was certainly not illiterate – seemed rather cultured and well-spoken, in fact – but much of what she said held very little merit or value to me. I resented her right away on so many levels, but what kept me from utterly despising her, I suppose – this woman whom I still didn't truly know or remember – was that at least she'd been honest about her disloyalty and greed. She had spoken the truth in saying she had never deserved my father, that much was certain.

Part of me felt a little sorry for her as well, to be honest. After all, I had never walked in her shoes; had never known what sacrifice and suffering she'd been forced to endure upon leaving a beautiful, modern city for a primitive, snake-infested jungle. And though I'd accompanied her on this journey, I still had no clear recollection of the times or the places she'd alluded to – though I'd hoped that her telling of it would have spurred my memory.

At least I'd inadvertently heeded her advice in that regard: to forget my old life as best I could. *That* I had accomplished in flying colors. I did feel compelled, however, to ignore her directive and try and track her down. But if I did manage to find her, what then? Would it prove to be a mission of rescue, revenge, reconciliation, or just plain suicide? Would it be worth the risk, both to myself and to others, to reconnect with my distasteful past?

Nor did the irony escape me that the answer to so many of the questions I'd been seeking had been within my grasp since day one.

My brain was hurting and my world was spinning; I knew I needed to get outside for some fresh air before my head exploded. I gathered the shredded remnants of my travel bag and shoved them back into the closet, slipped my mother's letter into my jeans pocket, and headed back downstairs.

Both Rami and Esmeralda asked me if I was okay as I strode, with forced calmness, to the front door.

"Yes," I assured them. "I just got this sudden urge to take a walk by myself. Maybe gather some shells along the beach."

"Okay, just don't stray too far" said Esmeralda in her usual motherly way. "It'll be getting dark before long."

Rami was inclined to accompany me, I could tell; but I signaled him, by a shake of the head and a wave of the hand, that there wasn't any need, and then headed out the door.

I strolled aimlessly along the shoreline for quite some time, allowing my feet to convey me in whichever direction they chose and for whatever distance they might prefer, while my racing thoughts strayed in a multitude of directions of their own. I was faintly mindful of the wailing of the seagulls and the slowly changing colors of the ocean's surface, as it dissolved from glistening orange to faded grey to a deepening slate while the opposing sun descended, until at length I found myself approaching the beckoning lights of my once-favorite tavern.

I paused before its rustic entrance, both tempted and hesitant to go inside; knowing a certain someone's glaring absence would only add to my loneliness and distress. My feet, however, which were still disconnected from my heart and mind, wound up carrying me inside.

The place seemed relatively empty; more forlorn than I remembered it from happier times. Reflexively, I glanced at my favorite booth ... and there, to my astonishment, sat Donna, immersed in some books just as she'd been on the very first day that I had seen her.

I floated, disbelievingly, toward where she sat, fearing her image would dissolve at any moment like the mirage of an oasis in a barren desert.

Thankfully, it did not.

"Do you mind if I share your booth?" I somehow managed.

She looked up quizzically from her book, appearing mildly surprised or perplexed to see me, and then glanced about the room.

"Well, I normally don't dine with strangers," she responded, "and it appears there are plenty of other seats about...but you do seem oddly familiar, so I suppose it'll be okay."

I wasn't sure if she was simply toying with me, or if she truly didn't recognize me. Certainly, my appearance had changed quite a bit, I considered, over the past many months. The last time she'd seen me I wasn't quite so tan, my hair was much shorter and less sun-bleached, and I hadn't any beard. I'd grown trimmer and more muscular as well, I supposed, and it probably didn't help that I'd neglected to remove my sunglasses. She, on the other hand, hadn't changed a wink; if anything, had become impossibly more beautiful.

"Thanks," I said, as I slid into the bench across from her.

"I'm afraid I may not be very good company, unless you prefer the studious, silent type," she said, flashing me that smile that could launch a thousand ships.

I sat staring at her from behind my shades, as though beholding some angelic vision; unable to remove my gaze from her hypnotically beautiful eyes. I'm sure it must have been unnerving to her, to some degree, but she casually rested her chin on her fists and then asked, "So what do you call yourself, my mysteriously silent stranger?"

Not a difficult question, ordinarily, but it caused me to pause and consider my response.

I thought about my circuitous journey: all the places I had visited, the people I had met, and all the beautiful friendships (including her own) which I had made along the way. About those people I had helped, who in turn had helped me begin to heal. About all those rich and colorful new images, the memories of which had begun to fill the void in my mind and soul. Suddenly it became clear to me that, in the process of searching for who I was, for a life that no longer existed, I had created an entirely new one, and that it really wasn't all that bad. It was just as Leo had predicted.

All of this passed through my mind in a fleeting instant, as I contemplated how best to answer her simple question.

In the end, I simply smiled at her and said, "Just call me John."

c

ABOUT THE AUTHOR

Forget about it